MW01714084

The Confession

by Remington Rose

Elmrose Publishing
Boston • New York

The Confession
by Remington Rose

Confessions is entirely a work of fiction. Any resemblance to persons living or dead is purely accidental. Any of the locations, institutions or people in this book that may seem similar to those in real life are also unintentional and do not bear any resemblance to locations, institutions or people mentioned in this book.

All rights reserved. No part of this book may be reproduced (except for inclusion in reviews), disseminated or utilized in any form or by any means, electronic or mechanical, including photocopying, recording, or in any information storage and retrieval system, or the Internet/World Wide Web without written permission from the author or publisher.

Copyright © 2003 by Remington Rose

For further information, contact the author at:
elmrose@katzmeow.net

Book design by:
The Floating Gallery
244 Madison Avenue, #254
New York, NY 10016-2819
(1-877) 822-2500

PRINTED IN CANADA

Confessions
Remington Rose
1. Author 2. Title 3. Fiction

Library of Congress Control Number 200310813
ISBN 0-9726779-1-7

Dedicated to children everywhere
past, present or future
who suffer abuse.

Acknowledgements

I am grateful for the loving support of my spouse and daughter. I thank Traci for her objectivity.

Thank you to Elmrose Publishing for making it happen.

Thanks to Lauren Talbot for her determinate ability to provide editorial supervision.

Finally, thanks to Andrew Ackers for his unique talent as an editor.

Chapter 1

LET ME MAKE IT CLEAR from the beginning I never meant to hurt her. Why it was her vulnerability which attracted me in the first place.

She was a bird with a broken wing. I held her captive in my cupped hands. Her little heart beating against my pulse; I felt her fear in my hands, even before I knew her name. From across the room you could sense her life force. Her very breath steamed the air.

I approached her with my mind first, never actually gazing up.

I was always good at feeding squirrels in the park. I would sit quietly eating my peanuts sensing them above me or on the wall before me. I would gaze away, holding them in my peripheral vision. Then I would drop a tiny peanut carelessly away from me and wait. I would breathe out through my mouth filled with peanut paste to reach out to them.

The scent was a hook cast deep into their senses. Oh, they would come, at last, right up to me, just as she did. Of course I absentmindedly reached into my pocket to get a tissue to begin cleaning my glasses as she crossed the room.

When my glasses fell in front of her she casually picked them up. I smiled sheepishly.

I call them my attitude glasses because they are just plain glass. For fourteen bucks they've given me a lot of mileage.

When she handed them to me, I quickly stuffed them in my breast pocket as if embarrassed to be wearing them.

She smiled radiantly when I did. I could see her reflection in the mirror. That's when I looked up at her.

She felt safe having a little advantage over me and it was my gift to her. You see, I wanted her to be at ease with me from the start.

My hook reached deep with little casting.

It wasn't her lovely red hair that attracted me or her deep green eyes, or the slight scar above her lip. Though I did like the way her lipstick seeped up into the crack of that scar. Her mouth, a sexual organ of magnitude, had this miniature labia to entice above; an apostrophe abbreviating a second crack.

Her velvet sleeves were scooped together mandarin style, but I knew. When she released them the left sleeve hung limp, not fully filled. Her grace of movement made me greedy to see.

This bird I could capture and train with little effort. Nature had fashioned her wing artfully to never heal. Where there should have been a hand only a single finger stump peeked out.

She would be mine.

She sat down next to me and waited for me to speak. I coughed nervously, but remained silent. She, of course, finally spoke.

"Are you all right?" she asked, almost whispering.

"Thanks, yes, just an allergy maybe . . .," I answered, modifying my tone to a whisper.

"Do you know the host?" she asked.

I didn't. I had just entered with several others from the elevator. It was a spontaneous decision. The laughter and music attracted me; maybe her scent was already in my senses.

"Great food," I responded. "It smells delicious."

"You haven't eaten? Would you like me to bring you something?"

Already she was serving me. I nodded and smiled.

She was back in a flash. She hugged the rim of the Styrofoam cup with her forearm and elbow; the delicate stump of her wrist peeked from her sleeve. With her right hand she carried a cup of fruit punch.

We talked together for two hours. Others danced; I decided to wait and not initiate this more physical gesture.

At about midnight the crowd thinned. I started rolling my sleeves down and putting on my sweater.

"Going so soon?" she asked.

"Well, I thought I'd go for coffee over at Max's Cafe. They have great pie . . ."

"My favorite's cherry," she answered.

"Then come on. Let's get some." I laughed easily, trying to look a little distracted.

So that was it: simple, really.

Chapter 2

AS IT GREW LATER, I offer to take her home. She hesitated. We took a cab so she would have less risk, not knowing me at all. I said my car was in the shop.

The brownstone she lived in was renovated. Looking up she pointed to the third floor.

"That's my window with the flower box. It's so mild this fall that the impatience are still blooming."

I didn't offer to walk her up. That would have been too forward. I shuffled a little, looked at my feet and laughed, which reassured her.

"Well, I hope I see you again soon," I whispered.

She didn't respond for a second then she offered, "We could go to the museum sometime."

So that was it really; a piece of cake.

You can't disguise the mind's inhibitions; they flicker across your face. There was a rippled turbulence to her face at times, an inner directedness she could not help.

Quite naturally I noted the moments they occurred. Our third time dining at Max's, a lady dropped a loose rose bouquet near our feet. Helen fluttered to pick them up. Her grace of movement concealed her impediment, yet a single thorny rose lanced her delicate wing. Without thinking, she pulled her stump up to her lips to suck the single droplet of blood. Then she let her sleeve fall. Instantly she was back on her knees retrieving the roses.

She was my rose. The red bloom on her stump was still visible.

Another time, on a walk along the embankment at Roosevelt Island, a child in a wheelchair moved toward the rail, a cupid doll in her hand. She caught her wheel on the cobblestone and struggled to get free. The doll dropped. Helen lifted the doll, smiled and unhooked the wheel to make it free again.

Each time her face blushed, the resonant nostrils flared and the transparent skin revealed her blood-engorged temple and throat.

At such times, she was at once revealed yet trying to conceal. She was captive to her own turmoil.

I was repulsed by her contorted face and seduced. Her pain was my harmony.

Chapter 3

I FOLLOWED HER FOR A few days to scan her pattern of movements.

I was discreet, she never knew. She walked her fluffy white dog at 5:00 a.m., then went back and showered. You could see the steam seep out through the open window. By 6:00 a.m. she was dressed again. The blinds were up. By 6:10 a.m. she was at Max's having cherry pie and coffee: two sugars with heavy cream.

I found an apartment nearby, a cheap walk-up with the bathtub in the kitchen, and of course I got a dog, a white fluffy one.

The first time we met with the dogs she called out to me from across the street. I looked up, straightened my attitude glasses and smiled. She waved and crossed.

Chapter 4

ALTHOUGH WE MET FREQUENTLY, I held myself back from any physical contact save a lingering kiss.

One evening while lounging with my head on her lap, I pretended. I turned my face into her lap so my hot breath would excite her. I felt her stirring; her own heat rising. I hugged her hips lightly but continued to breathe a deep dreamer's rhythm.

She trembled slightly, but I did not press my advantage; the stakes were too high. Later I drifted but she never moved my head from her fleshy pillow.

I awoke during the night. "I can't leave my dog Patty alone; she would whimper," I explained.

"Just tonight?" she asked hopefully.

I scrambled putting on my shoes, pausing long enough to douse my face with cold water.

"You could bring Patty here," she suggested.

My dear, sweet captive bird, so predictable.

Since I finished work earlier many nights, she gave me her apartment key. I prepared simple meals, sandwiches, soup, to greet her. I'd walk both dogs before she returned most nights.

⁂

ONE NIGHT WHEN she returned home, she found me huddled over my dog, its lifeless body in my arms.

The pillow which I held over Patty's face was quick and merciful. I was unable to be aroused for a long while, as I held its lifeless body.

She led me to her bed and gently removed my clothing and her own. She kissed my eyes and licked my salty cheeks.

I really was sad about the dog, but I saw a greater good in Helen's safety being secure with me.

Chapter 5

HELEN INITIATED IT. HER TENDER ministries included stroking my anatomy with her delicate stump. As she caressed my mouth I opened to hold it like a baby's thumb. I was tremendously aroused by this intimacy. I held her stump in my mouth, deeply in my throat. She orgasmed immediately, as I did.

She was an exquisitely formed creature able to be both male and female for me. Her potential was great but that night was only to build her confidence.

I would mold her into my perfect love. My tender vulnerable Helen who so loved to serve, would serve me. In exchange I would protect her from the cruelty of this world.

Chapter 6

HELEN WORKED DAYS AS A secretarial assistant. She rarely talked about it. I worked per diem doing editing mostly from home. She earned more than me but that didn't seem to bother her. It was during the daytime that I was able to regularly touch up my tinted blonde hair. I wore my blue contacts at all times except when Helen was out. Her friends were few but endlessly annoying. The answering machine recorded calls from Ned, Carol and Sally. For a while I allowed the female callers' messages to remain on the tape. But when Helen expressed interest in inviting them to meet me or going out with them, I realized it had to stop. They were interfering with her time with me, exposing her to worldly influences which could hurt her.

Soon messages came on the answering machine such as, "Helen, why haven't you called? Are you okay?"

A letter from Ned expressing his love and desire to see her I simply flushed down the toilet. I suggested toward Christmas that we change the telephone number. Several harassing calls had come in that disturbed her when I wasn't home. Of course, she agreed.

Chapter 7

HELEN'S MOTHER WAS IN A nursing home. She was withered and couldn't speak. Helen suffered seeing her mother with each visit. While Helen went down to get a coffee, I sat with her. I stretched the joining tube of her respirator so it would separate gradually from the oxygen tank. Helen held her mother's hand for the last time. Mercifully she died in her sleep that night.

Helen was hysterical with grief but her delicate system couldn't have dealt with the long, drawn-out suffering of these visits. She could devote her attentions to me entirely now and conserve her emotional strength. I would do anything to protect her.

That night I held her in my arms and rocked her to sleep. She called her job to say she would be out for a week. I sedated her tea heavily. She slept peacefully for two days except to go to the bathroom or drink some tea I had prepared. She slept naked, fully available to me as I wanted her. She was entirely mine now.

Her complete passivity and need for my help to drink, eat or bathe endeared her to me more. She was grateful and apologized, mumbling about how sorry she was to inconvenience me.

Her anatomy was a miracle of possibilities, even as I mounted her in her drug-induced sleep. I experimented but the days passed too quickly, and I soon tired of this game. She would be alert and ready for me when next we played, and of course, I could be patient. A patient, shy teacher. My flower would open to me voluntarily with time. I was now her only friend. I would honor her, not press my advantage. It would unfold as she allowed.

Chapter 8

When I was six, I entered the state hospital. There was nothing wrong with me but my parents were unduly concerned. I merely had a natural curiosity about nature and living things. Living on a farm gave me a laboratory of experimentation and observation. The chickens which were routinely slaughtered for food were my first subjects. My mom or dad would chase one down, grab it by the neck and chop its head off. I got the job of pulling its feathers out. The first time I observed this ritual, they went after Gertie, an unusual hen whose feathers grew irregularly long. I think she was graced with a natural mutation, which, had it been cultivated, would have yielded a highly prized show bird. Even her legs were a little longer and more feathered than most. I used to carry her around with me and sing to her, even teaching her to stand perfectly still to receive a treat from my hand. I once snuck down to my room in the basement with Gertie and slipped her under my covers. I fashioned a sort of diaper out of an old red bandanna, so my bed would stay clean. During the night I was afraid to leave her lest she cry out so I held my urine all night. Ironically, I wetted the bed, not her. In terror of a beating I awoke early, locked her in the closet and stripped my bedsheet to wash it in the basement sink. Then I replaced it wet and hoped it would dry before morning. I slept in the closet with Gertie until morning and let her out through the hinged basement window at about dawn.

Unfortunately, this separation from the group resulted in her being singled out for our next meal.

My mom brought me headless Gertie and told me to pluck her. I stood motionless. An ocean of sound filled my ears. Years later the psychiatrist explained this being my own blood rushing to my face, ears and head, so that it became audible to me.

I stood perhaps minutes or hours just holding Gertie's lifeless body nestled in my arms. My dad must have entered the room downstairs and screamed about the blood everywhere on me and the bed. He beat me worse than usual, but he couldn't pry my fingers off of Gertie's delicate torso.

I guess I must have been like that for a day or so. When the ambulance came I had soiled myself and Gertie smelled bad.

The injection made me sleep I guess. When I woke, I was on a cot in the state hospital. The doctor said I shouldn't have killed Gertie but I don't think I did. He said I fouled myself repeatedly and hadn't eaten for days. I guess they put me on intravenous feeding during that time. Anyway my clothes were gone, my room was gone, and so was my Gertie.

I WAS RELEASED a year later, "cured."

My parents seemed unchanged but glad to get me back. The beatings stopped for a while, but I never plucked another chicken again. There were more interesting things to study on the farm. Now that I was bigger I helped to milk the cows and goats.

Chapter 9

JENNY, A NUBIAN GOAT WITH long, silky black ears who gave us milk for cheese, was pregnant when I returned. She had one blue eye and one brown. Dad said her blue eye was dead from cataracts but I thought she was just special.

I began to worry about the baby she would deliver. Would it be sold or used for meat? Could it live out its days on the farm giving milk?

To study Jenny, I regularly dilated her womb, hoping to see the baby she would deliver. Once my dad caught me and threatened to send me back to the state hospital, but I wasn't afraid of him anymore.

I found I could fully grasp the baby's head with my bare hands if I first lubricated them with cooking oil. During one veterinary practice session, Jenny began to deliver.

It was a breach delivery, the legs first. I went screaming to my Dad who took over trying the delivery. It was still-born. Dad said the umbilical cord was wrapped round its neck so it didn't have much chance, although I suspected my experiments might have caused this. Jenny stopped seeking me out after this episode and died about a month later. Mom said maybe she was depressed about the "cub," or got infected. I figured it was my fault for touching her so much. But it also was Dad's clumsiness and unwillingness to call the vet.

These two incidents taught me about the preciousness of the female of any species.

I would find my own precious female someday and protect her from all harm.

Chapter 10

WHEN I WAS ABOUT SEVEN, I got the measles. I couldn't stop scratching and quickly was covered in bloody, infected sores. My mom cut my fingernails, but I still managed to scratch. She tried taping gloves on my hands. I managed to get the tape off so I could resume scratching. She finally tied me to my bed for several days and covered me with pink lotion. I thought I would lose my mind. The itching was so intense and I couldn't move to scratch. I screamed until my throat was hoarse. I guess I passed out as a natural defense. When I awoke, the itching had stopped and I was free again.

Chapter 11

THERE WERE VARIOUS OTHER RETURNS to the state hospital. Once my father caught me dissecting a pig. I had knocked it out so it would feel no pain. It was not much different from a doctor operating. Its insides were amazing. I held its beating heart and chronicled its reactions to electrical probes to its brain. My father and mother didn't understand my scientific curiosity, so again I went into the state hospital. I easily escaped and walked to the next state. An elderly couple took me in, no questions asked. I made myself invaluable on the farm. In exchange they fed and clothed me as their own son. When I ran from my home for good, it was to them some years later. I eventually enrolled in the local community college using my "adopted" parents' surname. When they died I inherited their property and life savings.

With little effort on my part I had been enfolded in a goodness and mercy I had never received at home. This independence of means, however modest, I protected by working after I received my associates degree. I found I had a gift for writing and editing and so I moved to the city, a short commute from my country home.

My adoptive parents had also graced me with a new identity. I applied for my social security number using their name from the will. I became "Dustin Caldron" their son and only heir.

I made few friends except for casual acquaintances, as my privacy was important to me.

Chapter 12

ONCE I DID FORM A short relationship with a young lady who worked as a housekeeper at night. I would often work the night shift too as there were legal briefs to be edited at night. I preferred night shift as my autonomy and privacy were ensured.

The young lady who worked at night was quite pretty except for a crudity of features due to a broken nose. She would leave me sandwiches and little gifts without her name. I felt sorry for her. She was sweet in a pleading, almost annoying way. When I finally mounted her it was on a desk with the blinds drawn. It was my first experience and very intense. She lay quietly a long time after I got up. I ran to wash her scent from me. When I returned she was crying. I held her close and rocked her. We continued for some time like this meeting only at work. She asked often if we might go to a movie or out on a date but I made excuses.

To my horror she became pregnant. I wanted her to get an abortion. She was afraid her parents would find out as she still lived at home. I confided in her that I was trained as a doctor's assistant and I could give her the abortion she needed. She finally consented. I was able to induce a spontaneous abortion with a bent coat hanger. I wrapped the fetus in some newspapers and threw it out some blocks from our place of business. She went home with several sanitary pads in place and a few stiff drinks in her system.

I never saw her again. I quit my job without explanation and moved out of state again.

Chapter 13

AFTER SEVERAL MONTHS, HELEN CAME home excited. "I've been promoted to area supervisor. I'll oversee the selection and final production of the children's books. Now we can buy a house," she said. She was flushed and her throat was splashed with blotches of dark red.

I wanted to grab her throat but I smiled.

"Well, where does this leave us?" I asked.

"Oh, I thought you and I would buy a house together, maybe, you know, get married?"

The veins on her temple were like worms. Her red hair seemed to catch fire.

My thoughts were racing. Could I purchase a house with my current identity?

Probably. I could just let her purchase it.

Marriage? Wouldn't I have to produce a birth certificate?

"Now slow down. The house is a great idea. Marriage, well in a manner of speaking we are already married," I said.

"Yes, but what if we want kids?" she said.

"Well yes, maybe in a year or so," I conceded.

Perhaps I could get a phony birth certificate. I had heard that people do. My mind was flooded.

"Let's just go one step at a time. You just got promoted. Get used to it before adding new stress like a house," I said.

"Oh, you're always so sensible," she said.

She cupped my face in her hands and kissed me.

The crisis had passed for now. That night I drugged her tea and played some games. My rage subsided as I saw her vulnerable and so alone on the bed.

She was still mine. She would do as I wished. She was really so much like a small child.

I would guide her. If she wanted a house we would get a house. She would be even more isolated. After all, she didn't like to drive. She would be dependent on me in every way.

Of course, all this would take time.

Chapter 14

DID I TELL YOU THAT Helen has very tiny feet? About a size five.

Her shoulders are milk white and soft and her hair falls in silk cascades of red, orange and blonde. Without makeup her lashes are tinted a deep brown and her cheeks have a bloom of rose. Her green eyes have flecks of hazel.

None of this matters compared to the delicacy of her wing. It is so silkily smooth and sensitive it gives me pleasure in unexpected ways.

Sometimes Helen slides her delicate wing through the cheeks of my buttocks with a firmness and tenderness of purpose that she has learned from my tutelage. She seeks to please me even when my requests frighten her.

Her breasts are like those of a pubescent teenager; erect, tiny and easily stimulated. The curve of her back and bottom tilt her back slightly. I can hold the cheeks of her tiny bottom with my two hands. She weighs next to nothing. Maybe eighty pounds.

When Helen is frightened, her eyes open wide and her lower lip becomes engorged with blood and trembles.

It is wonderful to see her fear and her mastery of it.

For she senses my needs. She senses that her abject terror will delight me too much, so she skillfully camouflages her fear.

But I know. I see the changes. Her chest and throat become red and blotchy. Occasionally a tiny tear forms at the corner of her eye. But she is stoic and determined to please me. If her lip trembles she purses it.

Dear sweet Helen.

I suggested we just use red ribbon to slightly restrict her movements. I fashioned a loose loop for all of her limbs save her wing.

The satin ribbon was lovely against her skin.

She lay quiet waiting as I studied my work.

Suddenly I was frightened. I wanted to grab her throat and strike her. I left the apartment and walked for several hours in the cold.

I got an ice cream sundae and read the paper. But I was aroused throughout this charade. I did grow calmer. When I returned she had fallen asleep or fainted.

I tenderly mounted her and released her bonds.

My dear Helen hugged me like a sinking swimmer. She screamed out once but I held my hand over her mouth. She couldn't help it.

She finally fell into exhaustion and I caressed her cheeks.

Chapter 15

ONCE I TOOK HER DANCING. She wore a green velvet halter with a wide skirt. When I twirled her the skirt fluttered up.

I could see the men looking at her tiny perfect body. They wanted to possess her, but she was my love. One had the audacity to ask her to dance. When I returned from the bathroom, he was spinning her and pulling her towards him. I remember I picked him up and carried him to the back of the dance hall. The rest is just a blur.

When I came back the music had stopped and the place had cleared. Helen sat in a corner, her wrap over her shoulders. Her skin was clammy and cold, so I took her home. She never mentioned the incident, but I never took her dancing again.

Helen and the little night shift maid have been my only experiences. In this way I am innocent too.

DURING ONE HOSPITALIZATION, there was some kind of incident. I was sore and bleeding for several days but what occurred I don't really remember.

One orderly used to wink at me so I thought maybe it was him but I'm not sure. He was kind of fat and smelled like rancid oatmeal. His front tooth was chipped and he was messy when he ate.

Several times when I was in isolation they put him in to watch me.

He would not talk to me. He would just take his one leather glove and turn it inside out and then poke his finger into it to turn it right side out again. He would do this very slowly and deliberately, over and over. He would lock his eyes onto mine and smile as he did this.

Once I vomited all over him; I was so repulsed by him. I laugh to think of it. I wish I could have vomited voluntarily in those days.

WE FOUND A tiny cottage-like house in Monroe, New York. It was inexpensive and had a fireplace and stone work on the side. I renovated the kitchen and bathroom easily. I am very good with my hands. The cottage was isolated and had an earth basement which needed work too.

Helen loved the town because it was small and quaint. The commute was fine. I suggested we keep the apartment in case we tired of domesticity.

Helen has an eye for color and selected rose burgundy and moss green patterns for most of the house. The house is set in from the road a ways and the neighboring houses are a good half-mile away on either side.

Helen should have known this was unwise.

As I have said, I never meant to hurt her, but she should have sensed the deepest stirrings of my imagination. Didn't she understand the creativity I could employ?

She was a big hotshot executive now, earning close to six figures. She dressed in mannish suits and wore her hair up in a severe French twist. She exuded confidence and efficiency at such times. But I knew her differently and she remained the same with me.

Several months later, she came home with her hair cut and blonde and I didn't recognize her. I think I stood with my mouth open for some time. My fists were clenched tight. I knew I couldn't stay . . . .

I paced the block like a caged animal for an hour and finally walked downtown. I think I must have walked twelve hours. My feet were blistered; I only had my slippers on. My fists were still clenched when I returned but she had gone to work. I took a hot shower and finally fell asleep.

She made a big mistake not coming home that night. Maybe she sensed my rage but she increased it all the more. Her dog Fluffy cringed under the bed and defecated on the rug. I kicked him only once but his nose bled.

I didn't sleep for two days. My nails had cut into my fists. I didn't eat or shave. I just paced.

FINALLY SHE RETURNED; she was, skeletal, a survivor of her own terror and my rage. Her hair was red again and she wore a tiny hair piece to lengthen it.

I wanted to extinguish her those many hours. Her pulse was evident at her throat. Her heart was beating rapidly and a gleam of oil and sweat appeared above her brow.

I lifted her, effortlessly. Fluffy came out to greet her. I kicked him aside.

I lay her on the bed and left the house.

When I returned my mood was considerably better. She hadn't moved at all from the position I had placed her in. Oh, my Helen knew how to please me.

I made her soup and fed her with a spoon. She ate averting her eyes. She was a pack pup who averts its eyes to defer to the pack leader.

I tilted her chin up so she could look into my eyes.

You know, I actually had tears in my eyes. Relief, for I desperately didn't want to hurt her. She placated me well, my Helen. She knew my inner workings. She was timid again. The whole experience would be forgotten after awhile.

I am capable of remarkable forgiveness.

If the days passed slowly I don't remember, but time took on a different flavor, more palpable. Each tick was evident to me. Sometimes, I could hear the ticking.

I was frightened. A caged animal, my muscles rippled with menace. My night shift editing job was easy. I was alone most times, or passed a nameless colleague occasionally. For the first time, I was frightened. I knew what I could be.

I took a male lover whom I abused cruelly. I paid him handsomely and raped him repeatedly with hard objects and my hands. Finally, my rage was abated. I gave him a dozen roses the night I left, and two dollars. I'm not certain why I did it that way, but I knew it would hurt him more than all the hurt I had already given him.

I returned to Helen as my old self again.

She said nothing. It didn't exist.

We were business as usual, although Fluffy never again approached me. I hated him, because he knew.

The house was a blessing, though. I could retire to my own space and this was good for our relationship. My favorite place was the basement. It had a sub-basement with a root cellar which opened out into the backyard.

I planted in that cellar. I finished the other parts, building a weight lifting area with large mirrors. When Helen was at work I exercised nude in front of the mirrors.

I watched my already well-developed body grow harder and bigger. My jaw became more squared and the cheeks of my behind were hollow where the muscle connected with the bone. I was lean: no excess, but bulky. I was getting ready for something.

I rented the movie Mighty Joe Young and watched it maybe a hundred times.

During this time I got promoted too. The company wanted me to come on days and supervise a couple of new graduates. I tried it for a while but disliked the necessary banter with co-workers. I explained that I needed my days for painting. I needed daylight to do my art. They finally agreed to let me go back on nights, but I kept my new salary. It wasn't all that much, but it brought our earnings close to the same.

Helen became pregnant the second year we owned the house. She didn't tell me, but her body was subtly different. Her pelvis tilted back more and her waist was less defined.

This couldn't continue. I could never share Helen.

I ACTUALLY DID paint for a while, but it revealed too much of me. I began during one of the state hospitalizations. Self-expression was encouraged by staff.

The last painting I did was when I was twelve. It was entirely in red. A body was on an operating table. The chest cavity was open and the heart was visible. I did a Hallmark card kind of heart. Many people who were larger were crowded around the table, a knife handle was sticking out of the body.

When my therapist saw it he put me on constant suicidal watch with the gloved monster.

I never painted again.

YOU JUDGE ME. Am I a monster?

I asked Helen to have an abortion. She refused. She denied that she was pregnant. She even showed me the pregnancy test, which read negative.

I paid an abortion doctor from the Lower East Side five thousand dollars to come to our apartment in the city. I sedated Helen in the usual way. He examined her and said she wasn't pregnant but I didn't believe him. He performed an abortion procedure to satisfy me.

He removed a clot of blood and threw it in the toilet while muttering.

Helen got infected and had to take antibiotics. She thought she had spontaneously aborted an early pregnancy, but she never suspected what really happened.

Helen said she'd never been pregnant before. She was very depressed. Her usually blazing red hair grew limp and took on a tinnish coat. It was growing back well and she stopped using the fake hair.

She had a greasy cast to her skin and her brow was smooth and shiny without the usual wrinkles of emotion. I remember when I worked in a nursing home for younger people with life threatening illnesses, there was this woman who was about sixty. Her hair was snow white and grew out in a dandelion halo. Her lips were always dry and cracked. Even her tongue was dry. I used to put glycerin on her mouth with a swab.

She would stare sightlessly at me. But her face: the skin was taut and smooth. No lines of tension from her previous life were visible. I think the muscles in her face were paralyzed but gravity couldn't pull or distort her face because she was so thin and lay flat always.

So it was with Helen. She was a smooth death mask. Her voice was a flat monotone whisper. She couldn't go to work, nor did she call. I called instead and explained she had suffered a miscarriage. They loved Helen so they gave her an extended leave.

I got really scared I had killed my Helen; mummified her somehow. It was never my intention to hurt her.

Finally, I found the name of a doctor and told him I was very depressed about my father dying. I told him I couldn't sleep and rarely got out of bed.

He recommended a mild antidepressant. I opened some vitamin capsules and emptied them. In their place I poured her antidepressant.

There was a noticeable difference within a week. Her cheeks again were flushed, and a smile flickered across her face.

I took Helen to Martha's Vineyard for a week. We brought Fluffy, who ran up and down the beach and even up a bushy hill. Helen packed several huge sweaters. April is still cold at the Vineyard. We had a cabin right over the water and in the evening we made a small fire and watched the sun go down. We had five nights of roasting marshmallows, drinking wine and making love under the stars.

Our last night Fluffy got caught in the bushes and I had to climb the sharp incline to yank him out. I actually had to cut his long fur with my Swiss army knife. He was tangled in a thorn bush when I cut him out. I tore my hands pretty badly. Fluffy lost his cute look for a while.

Helen thought I was unnecessarily rough in getting him out. But it was night. I could barely see and I was getting stabbed by those thorns. She's lucky I didn't cut his little heart out by accident. He could have strangled himself on his collar the way he struggled.

You underestimate my capacity for sensitivity. I might hate the little bastard but I couldn't let him choke up there.

When I came down my hands had bled all over his fur. She thought he was injured. She got hysterical with fear. My hands were hurting but she just held Fluffy and rocked him. Finally, I explained real slow.

"Helen, the dog is fine. I'm hurt . . . ."

Then she got with the program and put the damn dog down.

She licked my wounds and kissed my eyes and whispered tenderly to me. How grateful she was.

She was back.

During our second winter with the house, a storm blew out several of our windows. Hail stones rained on the roof and came in the windows. They were gray, the size of bullets and left small holes in some of the panes.

We were snowed in by morning. I put up plastic garbage bags temporarily, and we waited.

Three days later the municipal plows got us out.

The house was a real pain.

While Helen was at work, I cut new glass and hammered out the knife sharp shards that remained.

That's when all hell broke loose.

I got impatient and punched the glass out from one window and cut my wrist. Blood splattered everywhere. I kicked one of the windows I'd put in. I guess I started screaming and that's all I remember.

When I woke up, several hours had passed. I was covered in blood. I started to puke and shake. That's when I strangled Fluffy. He passed out but I kept shaking him.

I got nervous about my wounds and finally went to the hospital for stitches and antibiotics.

When I got home, Helen was back.

Okay, I made a big mistake. I should have set up an accident. But she believed me. I told her one of the panes of glass fell on him and cut him and I got cut trying to help him.

Frankly, she pissed me off by her attitude. I mean, which is more important, me or the dog?

I was so tired I finally must have passed out on the floor. She had cleaned up everywhere but around the dog.

Rigor mortis had set in and Fluffy was stiff as a board. I knelt down and pretended to sob for awhile. Then I scooped him up in my own sweater. I made a little casket for him and made a big deal about burying him.

Helen never said a word. She bit her fist until it was callused. The weekend was a complete washout. I went to four movies and ignored her, hoping it would pass.

I don't do well when I'm cornered. Hell, nobody does. Helen had my back against a wall.

I would have to get her pregnant. It was what she wanted. It would distract her from Fluffy and bring us closer.

Around this time I stopped cooking for us. Helen got really domestic. She bought an international cookbook. She would rise at 4:00 a.m. and cook. I'd hear her cutting vegetables or banging pots. I awoke to a house aroma of veal parmesan instead of bacon and eggs.

She was beginning to show signs but she didn't tell me. She didn't have to. Her face got puffy and her clothes fit too tightly.

I went shopping at one of those executive maternity places. I got her some suits and one dress.

It was a pisser with red sequins and a low neck but the balloon front.

I took her to dinner and she wore the sequin number. Her breasts swelled out obscenely and her behind jutted in the back.

But the sequins picked up the fire in her hair.

I began to be curious about the pregnancy. This wasn't a science experiment. This was my Helen.

I hope you understand.

I wanted to make sure she was all right. She began to have an inner light. She beamed. Fluffy was no longer on her mind.

She redecorated our bedroom and separated a space for a nursery. She set up a white bassinet and trimmed the edges of the walls on that side with carousel horses. She got a tiny lamp with horses which twirled around the bottom.

I got a silver baby spoon at Tiffany's and had it engraved "First" and placed it in the room next to the lamp. She blushed as she did when we first met and didn't meet my gaze.

I liked her saintly glow and her innocent expectation. She was a child herself. She was my child, created by me, to please me, to have *my* babies.

The scar on my wrist was receding, too. My index finger and thumb had lost some sensation but otherwise the hand was functional.

Around that time I decided to stop drinking. I was no alcoholic, but the blackout with the windows couldn't happen again.

I suggested that we go for the sonogram together. Helen cried. The baby was fully formed at three months. A tiny perfect being. It was swimming, the three-inch wonder was swimming in there on a long tethered umbilical cord.

I hoped it was a girl.

The doctor wanted to do an amnio, withdraw some fluid from the pregnancy and analyze it, "in case of hereditary birth defects."

I nearly smacked him. The arrogant man was tacitly implying that my Helen was "defective." My perfect Helen would have a perfect girl; I didn't care if both arms were missing.

I would be pleased in fact. Its spirit would be purer, closer to God if it was wounded.

To insure that the pregnancy continued safely, I did get a book on pregnancy. We pored over it together. We used a flashlight to train back and forth on her belly, so the baby could see it through her skin.

I sang to it.

I got some medical books and kept them in the basement.

I studied the gynecological pictures. How to do an episiotomy, what a breech birth was; it was all there.

I read up on drug interactions and pregnancy. The pills I had gotten for Helen's depression didn't pass the placenta. Hence they were safe during pregnancy.

I passed many a night checking the pregnancy. I even set up a workspace in the cellar. I got a massage table and added stirrups for Helen's feet. I sedated her, then faced her toward the mirrors in my exercise room.

I set up high intensity lamps.

We were in the "boonies," the wilderness, far from civilization. Oh, Monroe had a state of the art hospital but we could get snowed in after all.

What would my Helen do then?

I was very careful and respectful of her. I draped her just as a doctor would do. I wasn't going to let anything happen to her. My Jenny had been a casualty of my father's stupidity and arrogance. I couldn't risk the same thing happening to Helen.

The doctors were incompetent anyway. Whether she made it to the hospital or not, she would be safer with me.

I was not aroused by Helen's pitiable state; my altruism was.

I pulled back layers of tissue nightly to observe subtle changes.

She would awaken refreshed in her bed.

The eighth month while at work, she began contractions. Fortunately, they were Brackston-Hicks contractions. Her body was practicing for delivery. When she came home, I had set up our bed specially. I got a new white comforter and pillow covers with white lace to match. Cream and pure white, and I had made a lace canopy arrangement above.

I put chocolates by the bed and a bucket of chilled champagne. I put a double bouquet of roses on the pillows with a card.

"To my child bride," it read.

She cried tenderly. We toasted and made love all night.

I EXPLAINED TO Helen that she should take time off after the baby was born. I couldn't be expected to take care of a baby. It's not a chauvinistic thing. Get real. My natural curiosity could take over.

"We can't afford this house on one income," she said.

"So hang the house," was my attitude. It was the source of continuing stress for me and one thing I shouldn't be is boxed in.

The night she delivered she tried to conceal the labor. She just said, "I'm going out to a movie."

Come on, Helen, I thought, *you never go to a movie.*

"Shall I drive you?" I offered sweetly.

No response. So I began the car.

"Oh, never mind," she said. She dragged her left hand through a lock of hair and began twirling it. Helen never does this. It was a purposeful mannerism to set me at ease. Helen was trying to manipulate me.

Oh, I figured I could go along with this to see where she was going with it.

"I'm kind of sleepy anyway," I added. "I'm going to have a brownie and some tea and knock off for the evening."

Helen noticeably relaxed.

I got undressed and got in bed after sitting with my love for our usual cup of tea and blonde brownies. I had made them with crushed Valium and almonds. But Helen just picked. She did drink all the orange spice tea, though.

We lay down together.

In the morning I awoke in a panic. Helen was gone. So was the car. The brownie was in the toilet, vomited up. I had a kind of hangover. Helen had switched the cups. About five feet of snow covered the ground.

I was snowed in.

I went upstairs and threw open the window. By carefully climbing out and down, I was able to escape. No plows were in sight, but my rage was an energizer.

I left the house in my pajamas and parka. My work boots rubbed against my bare feet and one eventually got stuck under the snow.

When I finally got to the highway a Mack truck stopped.

"Mister, you alright?" the driver quizzed me.

"My wife, she went out in this storm. She's pregnant. She may have tried to go to the hospital alone last night."

"No problem, buddy, get in."

Well, partially I was freaking worried. Hell, she could be on the side of the road frozen to death. Or she might have delivered on the way.

Worse still, she had switched our cups of tea. Had she suspected? Or just made an error?

Helen could be dead. The idiots at the hospital wouldn't understand how to protect my Helen.

I thought I had the perfect plan.

When I arrived at the hospital, the driver squeezed twenty bucks into my hand and wished me good luck. I actually got misty, you know?

Helen lay in a narrow bed in puke-green sheets and wrinkled pillowcases.

On her bosom suckling was our infant girl. Her hair was pale blonde and her eyes were yellow hazel like a cat's. Babies don't smile at three hours, but she did. Her little crooked smile and unfocused eyes trained in my direction. The little bugger must have recognized my voice fromall those singing concerts I did at Helen's belly.

Helen was flushed and looked heavily sedated. Her breasts were engorged with milk and looked huge, white and delicate against the rosy lips of the baby.

I smiled in spite of myself. My anger melted away.

It had been a cesarean birth, which showed their complete incompetence, but fortunately Helen was all right.

At least her sexual parts were pristine and unscathed by birthing. She had named her Sara. Fine. I could live with that, although she had some nerve naming her without me. But as I have emphasized, I can be very forgiving.

Helen, they explained, would need to stay three to five days due to her sutures and her being a high-risk delivery.

The baby could go home immediately, however.

I explained that we had no help and that I had a night job. I also felt an aura of real danger to this arrangement. Anyway, I explained about the snow. "How can I get her home or continue the breast feeding?"

Finally, they relented. But the third day I had her bundled in a comforter and pale yellow snowsuit the size of a doll's. Helen had knitted it in secret. The matching bonnet made her head look like a daisy.

My hands and knees trembled as I bid my Helen goodbye.

"It will just be two or three days. You can handle it." She really meant it.

I had arranged for a nurse's aide from down the road to sleep over until Helen returned. She went to the hospital to place Sara on Helen's bosom and get machine pumped breast milk for our use at home.

I was a regular domestic genius.

Of course, I supervised all aspects of Nurse Helga's ministrations to my Sara.

Sara had a bloody vaginal discharge which scared me, but I was reassured that this was merely Helen's hormones affecting the baby and it would stop.

Actually, I was more ashamed by how the sight excited me. I became erect immediately at the sight of little Sara's delicate parts covered in the thin film of blood.

"I'll change her," I said.

My hands were trembling with delight. I figured if the nurse was present it was okay. I lingered tenderly, wiping out her delicately parted body and wondered if she could experience pleasure at this age. The nurse, seeing me lingering or being impatient, took over abruptly.

At the hospital, the sight of Helen breast feeding also aroused me. I wanted to partake of the milk and Sara's red lips over Helen's nipples gave me an almost voyeuristic feeling. I took lots of pictures of Helen and Sara and got them developed immediately.

I found by staring at them and shaking Sara as she nestled in my arms I nearly became aroused. I rocked Sara looking at the pictures in the dark in front of the television. I must have looked a vision of fatherly bliss.

THANK GOD HELGA was there.

Helen returned two days later but I was already in a deepening abyss. The patterns I had experienced during her absence I craved even when she returned.

She explained she would return to work full time in one week. I insisted we keep Helga at all costs, but she didn't understand, nor could I really communicate my worst fears.

I am not a monster. I reasoned that my love for Helen and the confusion between them was creating my overwhelming needs.

I was pairing Sara and Helen in a kind of sexual confusion. That was all.

During Helen's first night back I heavily sedated her tea. I gave Sara her last bottle, laced with a half teaspoon of Benadryl, an over-the-counter antihistamine which causes drowsiness. I did not want Sara to disturb my time with Helen. Believe me, Benadryl cannot harm an infant.

I needed my Helen to relieve my yearning and allow me to express my fullest self in order to protect Sara.

I set Helen up over some pillows face down. She was fully exposed to me. I focused a reading lamp to properly examine her. I needed to reassure myself she had not been violated by the doctors. Her delicate outer parts were as before. Using the surgical clamp, I opened her out and searched her innermost self. Her cervix was enlarged but only slightly. After all, the baby had come out by caesarean through her abdomen. I felt relief. Having removed all this, I mounted her. For the first time I wanted her simultaneously in front and back.

I plunged into her front while fully entering her from behind with several of my fingers. She was well lubricated. I respected the tiny unstretched tissue.

It would take time to open her for other possibilities.

I was in a frenzy. Although I came several times, I was unsatisfied. My anxiety mounted, as did my rage. I turned her over. Her long hair tussled over the cream and lace coverlet.

I caressed her winged stump and gently guided it into her. I was delighted. I rubbed myself against her until I finally fell upon her, satisfied.

The next morning I again begged Helen to stay home with Sara a little longer and let Helga stay. She didn't get it.

"Helen, the baby could stop breathing. There should be somebody with experience . . . The child is female. What will the neighbors think? I shouldn't be changing her diaper. You know."

I was patient. I all but spelled it out. Helen agreed finally to keep Helga three days per week. Things settled down for a while, but when the baby cried, Helen acted as though I didn't exist.

She would bring Sara into our bed to breast feed her and fall back to sleep. I explained to her that I couldn't share her. She just laughed and kissed my brow.

I lay next to Sara and my wife. My rage and excitement mingled. I could not behold them together without being aroused.

Most importantly, I feared my growing curiosity about Sara.

She was a miniature perfect Helen. Passive, delicately formed, with all the parts to delight like Helen and all the greater vulnerability.

One night, as I gently rubbed against Helen while Sara nursed, Helen awoke. She saw the state I was in. She gently removed Sara from our bed and returned to me. I was enraged and aroused.

She kissed me with all the skill and diligence she could. Lying passively, allowing her mouth to take in more of me, she accommodated me in every way.

I was rough, perhaps, or blind with a never-before unsatisfied ferocity.

Tears welled in her eyes and she cried out, but I continued. The more she cried, the angrier I became until I found myself slapping her. Her lip began to bleed and she became very still. It was then that I came with an intensity so great that I felt I would faint. I could see a kind of light behind my eyes and my gums seemed to vibrate. I guess I blacked out.

The next morning, Helen's left cheek was a little swollen and her lip was split, but it was very slight. She said nothing about it, but called into work sick. She told Helga not to come in for a few days.

She began to take sole charge of Sara after that, which frankly relieved me. I wondered if she suspected anything.

We hardly talked for several days.

Her figure was back and her face fully healed when she returned to work.

On the days Helga was there I read or slept. The other two days I enjoyed Sara.

I never hurt the child. I just explored her body. She was perfect in every way. I was able to cream her private parts during diapering and pause momentarily.

But I never violated the child; I merely explored as a scientist that gathers data might do.

She didn't seem to mind. So gentle was I that even as she slept without her diaper, I could carefully visit her. I left no marks as I inflicted no harm upon her. She was, after all, my darling, as Helen was.

Helen showed an uncharacteristic detachment around the third month of Sara's life.

She announced one night over dinner that she was going on a business trip to the Caribbean. It was a regional meeting for several divisions, as if I cared.

I explained that if she left, she would return to a dead Sara. I was quite matter of fact.

She stood up from the dinner table with her plate in hand, her body rigid and tears in her eyes. Then she let go of the plate; spaghetti fell to the floor. She stared at me. It contained a challenge, a plea, and a question.

"Did you mean that?" she asked.

She seemed to twitch as she awaited an answer.

But none came.

Then she walked over the spaghetti toward me and slapped me hard repeatedly across the face.

I started laughing.

She represented no challenge to me. I continued to eat. Again she slapped me. I grabbed her by the throat with my left hand and stuffed my face with garlic bread. I chewed it as I listened for that little gurgling sound in her throat.

Then I turned and yanked her head back with my other hand. I caught sight of Sara in my periphery. She was on the floor on the white lace quilt from our bed.

I suddenly felt Fluffy in my hands, limp and wet with blood.

Pushing Helen aside, I rushed over to Sara and held her against my cheek. I struggled to calm myself.

Perhaps I was too rough because Sara started crying. I put my finger in her mouth and began massaging her gums. Her teeth were beginning to come through and I'd seen Helga do this to calm her. I went into the kitchen and began heating a bottle.

Then I returned to the living room and placed Sara on my chest and leaned back in the reclining chair. She fell asleep with milk dripping from the corner of her tiny mouth.

Helen was still standing rigid, an hour later.

When I finally placed Sara in her crib and returned I round that Helen had lost her urine on the floor where she stood. She stared blankly ahead. I undressed her and washed her and covered her in the bed. Then I cleaned up the mess from the spaghetti.

Too much was at stake. I have endured more difficult moments than Helen's domestic nonsense, as a boy.

ONCE IN THE winter while working in the barn, I turned my ankle. I had taken a break to jump repeatedly from the loft to the soft bed of hay below. When I landed the third time, I caught my toe on a loose bridle in the hay and twisted my ankle. I tried to stand so I could limp home.

As I did, I caught sight of my dad. The barn door slammed shut. I heard the dead bolt slip across. Then I saw the shutters on the two windows close and heard them click shut as well.

It was not quite dark and the long shadows of evening would soon replace the tiny red slivers of light that filtered through the wooden slats. I was a prisoner again. The cold and wind howled outside until it was dark. Only a blue moonlight could be seen from where I lay on the floor. I could hear squeaks and scurrying. The barn rats were gathering momentum. I thought I felt one crawl over my leg and started screaming. I limped to the shutter and banged it. Then I used the pitchfork to pry at the shutter to no avail.

Finally the cold took hold. Snow came through under the spaces in the barn floor. First I was trembling and finally numb. Fear and fatigue mingled with hatred. I would stay alive if only to see my father one last time.

I imagined his head bashed repeatedly, his sides pierced with knives. I saw him a corpse, yet alive, clawing from within the closet in the basement. I saw me with a shovel throwing dirt and snow into his face. Only these images warmed me as I faded in and out of consciousness. He returned around morning, I felt his calloused grip on my shirt collar. He was slapping me repeatedly to rouse me.

He dragged me through the snow to the house where he left me on the kitchen floor. He clapped his hands together, downed his remaining coffee and trudged out, slamming the kitchen door.

So windy was it that even his vigorous slam left it open. I finally closed it, blinded by blood, tears and rage.

I NEEDED TO maintain my characteristic distance and altruism with Helen and Sara, or they could both be dead.

I began to reflect on Helen's subtle but consistent personality changes. Perhaps she had switched the teacups that night she left for the hospital. She had, after all, left without me for the hospital.

She was returning home sometimes an hour late in the evening. Admittedly, the commute was long. But I needed to reassure myself about Helen. I paid Helga to come in additional days and went into the city to observe Helen's movements.

She arrived at work punctually at 8:00 a.m. and left each day at 4:00 p.m. She went to lunch two or three times a week with a co-worker. He was balding, fat and wore thick glasses. He would gallantly open doors and pull out chairs for her.

Once they went into a French restaurant for an hour and a half lunch. They came out laughing and walking closely in synchrony.

He walked Helen to her car at four that day, and climbed in. They sat for a long time inside before he got out.

I could smell cigarette smoke in her hair that night, probably from him. I'm not saying she was fooling around, but she was venturing too far from a safe distance. She was walking a razor thin course away from me. I had to put a stop to it.

I was patient by nature.

When the worst winter snow watch was beginning, I hammered large nails into his back tires. Maybe nothing; maybe pay dirt. I also punctured his fuel line, leaving a slow leak. On an icy evening, maybe destiny would take over.

A few days later, Helen was late again and the cigarette smoke smell again lingered in her hair.

This time I found him coming out of a bar after work. He was as drunk as a skunk. He passed out puking. He never saw me. I came up from behind him. I broke both his knees in an alley. I was home two hours later, before Helen.

Good old Helga was a great help.

I was actually very calm and this time I remembered every detail clearly. This jarred my memory as I drove home.

Few times stand out in my mind with the clarity of my thirteenth birthday.

I had been drawn to the attic of our old farmhouse in the spring because I could hear squirrels running back and forth. No doubt they were setting up house in the strewn debris and old blankets that wrapped photographs and suitcases.

The ladder to the attic pulled down from the ceiling with a rope. The stairs were well rotted and barely held my large frame as I mounted.

When the squirrels heard my steps on the hollow boards across the beams, they fled.

I inspected the corner they ran from. I found an old valise, well dusted, but hidden somewhat under stacks of newspapers and magazines.

One bundle of magazines were new. As I flipped through the pages, I found layouts of young boys and girls in various states of undress.

One picture was browned from age and shoved in among these. It had been folded and unfolded so many times it was beginning to rot and separate. It depicted a blonde child, perhaps seven. Whether boy or girl could not be determined by the face or torso. But the position of the legs greatly revealed it to be a boy.

The eyes appeared to be taped shut and the arms bound together. It seemed a home photo somewhat out of focus.

Though there was little light filtering through the one dirty windowpane, it was enough to see that the child seemed genuinely strained and not posed. I squinted to study its various parts in horror and excitement.

I began to look through more of the magazines, finding more gruesome postures than my young mind could have imagined.

My excitement mounted although I was also nauseous. I do not know to this day if fear of detection or repulsion finally caused me to vomit. But I threw my head out the tiny window and retched in dry heaves for some time.

When I was calmer and less nauseous, I began to look through the valise. It appeared to contain ordinary sepia family photos from long ago.

Only one which was among them again seemed to have been folded and unfolded numerous times. This photo of the same boy showed him exposed from the back, his small buttocks marked, perhaps by a stick, a hood over his head.

He seemed the same boy as the previous, so I laid them side by side to compare the square boniness of his shoulders and the way his pelvis protruded, even his size seemed the same.

Again I retched and vomited. Fearful of being caught, I carefully placed both photos back where they had been hidden and began poring further over the newest magazines. Some were similar to ones I had seen at newsstands in town, but several were violent postures of nudity, depicting victims in distress or hooded. Sometimes a hand or object was shown. Sometimes partially nude figures were abusing them. I got excited by these pictures and began touching myself. Finally, as it grew darker, I could no longer study the photos so I just lay back with the memory of them.

Thus, when I heard the attic stairs pull up, I panicked.

My father stood above me in his work boots, his large brimmed hat tilted back, his toothless smile below. He was hitting his hand with a leather whip which had several tails and looked well worn from farm use.

I gasped for air but felt none enter my lungs.

He sprung at me rapidly yanking my head back and stuffing newspaper in my mouth. I started to choke and cough. He tied my hands behind me and kicked me.

Then he yanked me to a standing position.

To my horror, my pants were still down from my self-explorations. He could see what I had been doing and worse, he could see my swollen, pitiful privates. He yanked my pants part way up and began to hit me with the whip.

He surprised me because though it whistled through the air it landed softly around my face, neck, and chest. Then he began to train the whip toward my privates. First he hit me gently, then harder, then gently. It was both painful and stimulating. Instead of shrinking from fear and disdain, despite myself I became excited.

This humiliation caused me to rebel against his abuse, but he shoved me hard against the beams again. When the newspaper eventually slipped from my mouth, he simply smiled and brought his finger to his lips for me to be quiet.

I was quiet because as much as I feared what was happening, the fear that my mother or any other might see me in this condition was greater.

He continued to whip me gently around my thighs, buttocks and privates until I fainted.

When I awoke, I was in the basement on my cot, my underwear was bloody and mixed with semen. Was it my own or his? I never ventured until now to guess. I only know that I planned his future that night.

HELEN SHOWED NO change after her lunch-buddy was inconvenienced. But I initiated a conversation about returning to the city and resuming the full time use of our apartment.

Lately, Helga had been missing days with Sara and announced she was unwell. She would need surgery and a lengthy recovery. My Helen had been almost uninvolved with Sara. She left for work at six every morning and often returned when Sara was in bed.

I was beginning to be the sole caretaker. I reasoned that this was unnatural and unwise. Helga had been a buffer, but without her in this desolate house, too many ghosts could exert power over us. If we were in the city, Helen could leave later and return earlier. We could arrange for childcare more easily. We could meet other parents and children in the park.

I doubted that even our neighbors knew we had a child. For that matter, I doubted they knew about Helen, as she was rarely at home or with us during the day.

Helen was opposed to this idea.

"This is my dream house. Someday it will be Sara's. We may want other children. This is a more wholesome environment than the city."

She agreed to negotiate an extended leave or flex time hours so she might go in only three or four days per week. We agreed that I even might take a weekend editing job so she could cut back to part time hours.

I explained that I also was concerned about her safety in the city as she was there until dark.

"You must know people who have gotten mugged on their way to their cars or after work before they even make their way home— men and women. Helen, I'm concerned for your safety . . ."

She was noticeably pensive; you know what I mean.

Why, you may ask, did my lovely Helen stay with me?

Pathologically low self-esteem; a traumatic youth?

I know nothing of Helen's early beginnings. Of her mom, whom I met briefly and she was too far-gone to know. No mention was made of her dad, nor of sisters, brothers, uncles or aunts.

I am too discreet to probe. What she volunteered, I would have accepted at face value. She gave me nothing.

But the omissions; do they not tell more than well-constructed myths? The silence, utterly and simply, told me more.

Indeed, Fluffy was more to Helen than all of those who may have existed or been hoped for. Certainly, Fluffy was more than mother or embodied a generic family of equal strength and depth as anything we might understand. For I could also measure the depth of her attachment by the depth of her despair when Fluffy died. Fluffy was her sibling, her first child, her trusted friend.

Perhaps that was why finally I detested him so. As I have said, I cannot share Helen.

WHY, YOU MAY ask, do I stay with Helen? I am good looking; physically tall, muscular, with an inherited wealth to offer a safety net to future partners.

Helen is my perfect child—my better self—the perfect foil to my rage. For until now she has only answered with love, gentleness and mildness to my irrationality, my madness.

Do I admit to madness? By your standard, not Helen's.

Does she fear to leave me?

Of course, but that is also her attraction to me.

I am her final authority in all matters. She feels in me—well, yes, a sort of god. She senses her safety. For as a god of power, of control, I allow little of what is real to affect Helen. She remains in a perfect "Sleeping Beauty Limbo."

Not quite awake—not quite knowing. She is protected from decisions—from anxieties or self-doubt.

She experiences also godlike power over me, for she controls me equally with a faultless surrender to my will.

Occasionally, of late, she has rebelled. I fault this town, the hours away from my influence and the long commute. But I give to Helen what she needs to continue to serve me. My dilemma now is Sara and the house. Can Sara continue with us—safely or at all?

Would our simple world be better maintained in the apartment?

I go day by day. I sense her pulse, her needs. For although she is mine to control, to serve me, I must not destroy her. I must not harm her mortally or pierce her soul. She is the only one I have ever trusted, loved, or come to. She is all that is pure, good and noble, all that I would be. By preserving her perfection, I redeem my own soul.

What can you know of an animal who craves blood, lust, revenge; who can love utterly and selflessly one tiny, wounded woman?

For on the day I destroy Helen, I would have to destroy myself.

Chapter 16

WHEN I PURCHASED THE RIFLE, it was as a youngster in the deep country with two ailing foster parents. I did not need a permit. After all, as property owners deep in the woods, protection of private property was expected and indeed wild animals regularly prowled areas near domestic ones.

Fortunately, I have never tested it nor do I hope to but since I must protect our little home and family, I retain it in an antique golf bag in the closet. I don't expect I'll ever need it.

As I believe I have mentioned, on my thirteenth birthday I began to plan for my father's future.

A hunted animal catches the scent of the hunter. It may not turn to pounce until a split second within its own death. Then nature decides the weaker—hunter or prey.

For two years I worked quietly next to my father feeding chickens, plowing fields, repairing fences. Content to wait for heavenly aspects to converge.

When the plow hit a large rock, dad just got off and lifted it out the way as he usually did. This day its sharp edge tore into the back tire, the motor still raging. He stepped out to remove it. As he climbed back in I quietly pointed to the deflating tire. He leaned off center of his seat to look. Then I pushed him, momentarily plunging his left arm, the one which had whipped me, into the thrashing blades.

Blood splattered. I jumped down and backed off. He stood aghast, looking at what remained of his arm. I began to run in the direction of the farmhouse. It was reasonable for him to suppose that I ran for help. I did not.

When I entered the house, I lifted the telephone receiver and held it to my ear, poised, ready to begin a distress call.

Mom was not in the house so no confrontation was necessary. I waited perhaps a half hour, then placed a call to the doctor in town. I was only fifteen and this seemed a reasonable thing to do.

"Dad's been hurt in the field; come quickly!" I said. "His hand is hurt."

The doctor came immediately but it was a good half hour's journey from town.

When he arrived, we ran to the field. Dad had passed out and gone into shock. He convulsed several times before we stopped the bleeding with a tourniquet. "The use of a tourniquet is a decision to forfeit the limb below," the doctor muttered.

Dad never recovered consciousness, although we drove almost an hour to the Medical Arts Building in town. He convulsed many times before going into a coma.

The insurance was helpful in paying off the mortgage on the farm. I presumed mom managed just fine without him. Not long after that, I left.

Chapter 17

JOSIE WAS HER NAME. As I have mentioned, I decided to give up alcohol because I needed to be in full control. Yet that night I followed Josie some ten blocks through Manhattan into McCauley's Bar.

She was underclad in mid-winter. She wore only a nearly transparent silver metallic dress. A sleeveless tank top revealed her thin arms, ornamented with a cheap bicep bracelet.

Her nails were crimson and long. Her legs seemed bare in worn down clogs, which accentuated her height. Her hair hung loose in waves cascading down her back and shoulders.

She sensed my attentiveness and changed direction to follow me and pass me on the streets. It was two in the morning. So thin was she that her firm buttocks were dimpled where the muscles met at her hip. I could smell her armpits and her female parts. She appeared homeless, yet immortal.

She paused abruptly and turned to me. Her black hair contrasted starkly with pale blue eyes. This too added to a sense of her unreality.

Her lips were full and very red. "Could you spare some money? I need a manicure," she began. It was a demand based on a soul-felt necessity. Then she smiled a smile so filled with sadness.

"My teeth, I must fix them soon. Do you not see the gums are bad?" She pulled back her teeth in the smiling grimace of death. She was a skeleton of breathtaking beauty. I gave her a twenty. She continued to walk before me, a goddess.

Her feet were black and the soles worn from too many walks.

"You will call my mother: 555-8686 and demand my inheritance. I cannot be locked up. I must be free. I will not let them handcuff me again." She had a Spanish or European accent. I believe she fabricated it.

I offered her my coat and she looked with disdain at it. "This is not my style. I am meant for furs, gold, jewels."

She continued to walk. When she entered the bar, so did I. Beers are not hard liquor, I reasoned.

The bartender knew her. He brought her Tequila with salt on the rim and a hard boiled egg.

I sat several seats away from her so I could study her entirety.

Her twig-like arms bore scars from needle marks, perhaps old. She threw her head back and laughed heartily. I could see her bony chest and perfect breasts. The nipples were hard from the cold. I could make out her front, I thought, despite the darkened bar. She wore no underwear.

"I need black velvet pants, gold hoop earrings, many gold bracelets . . ., " she said to me.

I moved closer to her. She needed a bath. She could have AIDS or syphilis or lice. Yet she looked darkened mainly from prolonged exposure to the elements.

"Come to my house and bathe and tomorrow I will get you what you desire."

"Now, in the Village; NewYork never sleeps. Horatio Street. They hold for me my outfit."

I paid the bill. Now three in the morning, we walked further amidst transvestites and sado-masochistic vamps. Her store was garishly lit up.

"Back so soon, Princess?" They handed her a black feather boa scarf, velvet leggings and a bolero jacket, all black.

She put them on without looking in the mirror.

She was stunning.

"I need gold earrings and bracelets," she demanded, a petulant child queen.

The counterman brought out several gold bangle bracelets and large hoop earrings. He assisted her in placing them. She tossed her head, first downward then back, fluffing her hair out.

"Tomorrow a manicure."

Although we had walked some six miles, she was invigorated and still seemed unaffected by the cold.

The old apartment Helen and I originally shared was empty. Helen was in Monroe, now having taken the prolonged leave of absence I suggested. Here I was alone with my child queen.

"You let me wash you with this lice shampoo, or no manicure."

She laughed a bitter, rebellious laugh and spat at me. I slapped her hard and locked the door from the inside with the key.

She stood fierce. Her eyes were fire. Her lipstick, slightly smudged, made her look vulnerable. I grabbed her thin arms behind her and slipped a pair of handcuffs on. She kicked and spat and butted with her head, so I bound her legs with her own pantyhose.

Then I drew a hot bath mixed with lice shampoo and lifted her in. So what if she was dressed. The stuff would work anyway. I scrubbed her face and hair and clipped her toenails which were also red. Then I lifted her out onto the bathroom floor and dried her.

"You scum, you've ruined my outfit," she screamed.

I slapped her and lifted my finger to my lips. "Tomorrow, a manicure and a shopping spree. You are more beautiful than Cleopatra."

She tossed her head but seemed satisfied. Then I removed all of her bonds. Because of her thinness, her wrists were cut, but I put some peroxide and dressing on them. Then I asked her if she would like a drink. She walked barefooted in the thin, already drying clothes, inspecting everything.

I poured her a cognac and crushed a Valium into it. I poured myself a double. She gargled with it, then she drank it as an old Marine might, in two or three gulps. From her purse she pulled a red fuchsia lipstick and reapplied her color.

Her pelvic bones and pubic hair were visible through the thin, silver metallic dress. Her thighs were narrow as an adolescent boy's. She seemed almost to be a boy in drag, save the perfect breasts. They were large and firm, more ample than such a ruined body could expect to have. I wondered if they were silicon marvels.

She was the most fascinatingly repulsive creature I have ever met—a feral cat I had captured. So many before on the farm had managed to escape, but she seemed content to stay.

After all, what choice did she have? I had the key and the lovely cognac was a mellow lens to see me more pleasingly.

I picked her up and lay her on the bed.

I asked her if she would like another drink. She drew her legs up and gripped her knees. Her toes sparkled in the dim light. One middle toe had a tiny jeweled ring. I could plainly see her body without the underwear in this position.

She passed me her empty glass. I gave her a refill of the same. Her eyes glowed glossy high and insane. She emptied the next in smaller sips. For each sip she pulled her hem a little higher. I sat opposite her in the winged chair. She thought she was in control. I liked this.

I found it hysterically funny and also sad.

I leaned back and studied her. She let one shoulder strap of her dress fall and tilted her head. She was a practiced dancer on this stage. This was choreography she had perfected in many previous performances.

I rose and slowly approached her. I entered her fully dressed, even my work boots were still on. She became too wild and scratched me. I put a pillow over her face until she passed out. The alcohol and Valium alone should have done this.

She was so thin. It was difficult to enjoy her skeletal body. She was dry.

I lubricated her and straddled her. I shaved her pubic hair off. This was truly amazing to see. She was just a little girl now, her hips barely budding in puberty. Yet the silver streaks in her hair hinted at a woman in her forties.

She pleased me enormously. She was at once wild and totally frail. She awoke during the second visit I paid her.

Her strength and disorientation made her difficult to control. But then I turned on the light and stroked her head and reminded her we would get her more gold bangles tomorrow.

She hissed at me in disdain. I brought her a third drink. She emptied it quickly. Then she cooperated fully with any and all I wanted.

I had gotten one of those toys they sell that fits into the back and front like a chastity belt and locks. It comes in various sizes to stretch and stimulate your lover at all times. In this way, whenever I wanted her, she would be ready and in fact suffering to receive me. It cost me twenty-five dollars at one of those sleaze shops in the Village.

Seeing it on her delighted me.

When she awoke she was naked, save my lovely gift to her. "If you are sweet," I said, "and wear it all day, I will give you whatever you want."

She drew back her teeth. "I need the dentist and a manicure."

"Fine. Then you shall have it."

I took her to an inexpensive jewelry shop in the diamond district and got her more bracelets, then I waited while she got a pedicure and manicure.

She refused to eat. As far as I could tell, we had been together thirty-six hours, and she had only had those drinks. "Let's go back to my apartment," I said.

She was hesitant. She let me put a long, wool cape over her shoulder midday, but she was still under-clad.

I said, "I have a special present upstairs. A surprise upstairs."

Her eyes glimmered slyly. She squeezed her own nipples through the metallic dress. We went upstairs. Again I locked the door and as she turned to see me, I slapped her repeatedly until she was unconscious.

I broke several Valiums and placed them under her tongue. They would be absorbed and dissolved in this manner without her choking.

She was becoming tiresome, but I was curious about my little chastity belt experiment.

I unlocked the leather fastening and slipped out the two lubricated intrusions from her body. There was no blood. Just a slight chafing from the leather and some clear bruising at the entrance to both openings.

This was to be expected as she was so thin.

I loved the bruised, blue cast of her shaved body. The marks of pain she had borne all day for me. I wondered if she had been excited or merely greedy for my gifts.

She had not complained.

This would be our last tryst. She was not, after all, my Helen. I had been absent two days. Helen would be hurt, no matter how clear my excuses.

She was definitely more relaxed, not just by the Valium but her inner muscles were much enlarged, even by this short period of stretching. I would never forget her. She was a gift to me from God. She made me realize my true power and destiny.

I contemplated returning to her again and again to enjoy more mind games. But it was risky.

When I finally roused her, she smiled stupidly. I fed her scrambled eggs, but she spat them in my face.

I gagged her and left her on the bed, just her legs cuffed and her lovely belt back on.

I went to Central Park and fed the pigeons and called Helen.

"Sara," she said, "is asking for Daddy. Helga came by and is willing to return to work."

"I'll be home in two days," I said abruptly. I hung up, confused.

I went to the Zoo and watched the seals and monkeys and got several helium balloons.

When I got to the apartment, Josie was dead. She had vomited and choked. I removed the chastity belt and dressed her.

It was two in the morning when I walked her thin body out into the street. I supported her at the waist. I just kind of glided her along. She seemed drunk at worst. I walked over to the West Side Highway under the docks and gently slid her down. There was no evidence of foul play. She was a drunk, homeless woman who had choked on her own vomit. I removed all the articles of clothing I had purchased for her and took them home. There I sterilized them. The cape and boa I had dry cleaned.

The leather chastity belt I kept.

The gold earrings and bangles I had gift-wrapped and brought home to Helen with a dozen roses.

Chapter 18

HELEN THANKED ME FOR THE presents, but they really didn't suit her. She was delicate and tiny. Such jewelry was vulgar looking and too heavy to suit her.

She just put them aside in her jewelry box. The roses she put in the center of the living room and made a frequent fuss about sniffing.

No mention was made of my absence. I muttered about staying at the apartment in the city and long hours at work, but it really wasn't necessary.

Sara looked bigger to me; round and more elongated. Her smile now had five teeth.

Helen had had her ears pierced which was a mistake, but I said nothing. I can be quite patient.

For now, my lust for Sara seemed abated, for which I was grateful.

You know self-determination is the true mark of a great people coming into their time.

I, too, felt more than ever to be self-determined, the mark of a great man. God, if there was a God, definitely was with me. My power and confidence was growing each day.

I felt empowered for a special destiny.

Thus, when Helen suggested we begin attending church in town, I embraced this.

When we dropped Sara at the nursery before service, I was unnerved to leave her with strangers. However, my chest heaved with more breath and energy than usual. My blonde hair, newly colored and cut, gave me a professional air. I even put a matching handkerchief in my breast pocket to go with my new yellow tie. If respectability was her thing now, I could handle it.

Being under the scrutiny of this pretty small town could not ruffle my feathers.

As we sat in church, the light of the stained glass seemed illuminated from within. I wondered if my face perhaps glowed too. Surely my powers to discern were sharper than ever.

Helen wore her emerald velvet cape. She looked like a Victorian lady. She even wore a black velvet muff in which she cleverly hid her little winged arm.

Just to please me, she had worn one gold bracelet I had given her.

The sermon was something about Jesus bruised for our sins. Unfortunately this flickered an unexpected image of Josie's bruised body.

I sang, with gusto, songs from my childhood on the farm. I remembered for the first time my dad taking me to church, my hair slicked back with butcher's wax and my pants carefully ironed by my mother.

Mom never came. She would make baked beans, bacon, toast and eggs. The aroma would greet us before we stepped through the door.

On such occasions, my father seemed a kind of proud peacock. He was oblivious to us, just playing out a drama in his own head about his superiority and rightful place in his household and the community.

He wore polished knee-high riding boots, a brown suede vest, and a coarse tweed jacket with suede patches on the elbows. He was the proper country gentleman.

I stood stiffly by his side, daring to look up only fleetingly at those who might address him.

He even put his arm around my shoulders during the service. His back was ramrod straight without benefit of the hard pew bench.

Leaving, he would shake the minister's hand. Once I chanced to look up at such a moment. He squeezed my hand too tightly, smiled his thin lipped, bloodless smile, and pushed me aside.

So here we were again as they say, "in God's house," Helen and I.

After church, Helen wanted to go to coffee hour but I emphasized getting Sara home.

Helen was more beautiful than I remembered her. I studied her as she cooked us lunch. Her hair gleamed; her teeth were more white. Her tiny barefoot feet were neatly pedicured.

A calmness had settled over our household. I no longer felt the fear of remaining in this isolated setting.

Sara ate her lunch on my lap easily able to munch a piece of bread with her gums and teeth.

The house was somehow different to my eye. A tiny Tiffany's lamp perched on my computer table was new. A pair of praying hands on the kitchen wall contained the Serenity Prayer. The floor was polished to a high gloss. Helen had been busy in my absence.

Well, good. I would also be a picture of serenity.

I worked in the garden after lunch and changed a bulb in the cathedral cut hallway. I cleaned out the house gutters and finally as night fell, settled back into our "Norman Rockwell" picture.

Helen nestled in my arms that night. Pristine clean, my angel allowed me any privileges I desired. She was both separate and part of me. My wishes and her personhood were one.

Mastery was no longer necessary with her. So cautious, tender and vigilant was she to my will.

I fell into blissful sleep as I never before knew was possible.

Chapter 19

THE WEEKS TO COME WERE filled with chores, getting ready for a Spring vacation and Sara's new accomplishments. She was playing with toys and squeaking rattles. A photo album in pink and rose contained memorable moments from our daughter's first few hours to the present.

One day in a shopping mall, I chanced upon a tiny gold cross and put it around Sara's neck.

Therefore, I was taken back breathless, a gut punch delivered unexpectedly when I returned home one afternoon to find my little wonder with her nails painted red and the black feathered boa on the floor next to her.

I think I staggered. I swooned and awoke to find Helen on her knees with a cool compress on my head.

Spring was in the air and a Hyacinth plant made me nauseous with its aroma.

"You're overworked," she said.

She helped me into the recliner.

I went to the inactive bar area and poured my first whiskey in months.

My hands were trembling with rage. My face was hot, my throat constricted. When I tried to speak, it was only a croak.

Perhaps minutes or hours later, I was able to compose myself to speak.

I whispered. "Helen, remove the red nail polish from Sara's nails." Nothing more was said.

During the night, I lifted the black boa from its tissue box in the closet. I had forgotten about it. Its aroma sickened me as the Hyacinth had done.

In the cellar, I burned the box and boa in the sink and ground its ashes with my heel into the moist earth below. To have perfectly forgotten then remembered was a shock to my soul.

My resurfaced rage was also a shock. So domestic and idyllic had these months been. I had been lulled into an almost Messianic view of myself.

Helen's alarmed expression and trembling hands were sufficient information. I had shown my rage utterly. Her temple, the wormlike veins pulsing, her speed a testimony to the urgency of my whisper. She never waivered but immediately lifted Sara from my sight to a safe distance upstairs.

Hours passed silently, her upstairs and me below. Finally, I knew I must go, at least for a few days.

The New York apartment, unventilated from my last visit, was suffocating. I, who am normally stoic, vomited, even as I had those many years ago in the attic room. I heaved dry and retched over the toilet, finally passing out on the filthy sheeted bed.

When I returned a few days later, Helen was packed for our vacation. We would return to Martha's vineyard but to a different house.

Sara was walking with one hand held.

The weather, far from warm, was crisp. Colors were shifting to a rainbow palette.

Days were longer. Helen surprised me by packing knitting.

All the while we were there, she used evenings to knit. It was a little blanket with the colors of spring. I assumed it was for Sara. Then I began to study her figure. I explored her in every way. To my horror, she seemed pregnant again.

I confronted her on our third day at the Vineyard.

"And baby makes four . . .," I cooed.

She looked down; a tight smile and clenched jaw were my reply.

Mysteriously, about a week after our vacation, she came home tense and thin-lipped. She brushed passed me and sat down in the recliner. She began ripping out the stitches in the nearly finished comforter. She methodically rolled it back into a ball. Then she went to bed. That night, when I tried to hold her she stiffened. In the morning, I found soiled sanitary pads in the toilet and a bloodstain on our sheet. I don't know if she spontaneously aborted or went to the doctor.

She again lapsed into the ominous depression I had seen some three years earlier. She would not pick up Sara.

She stared blankly ahead and missed several days of work. I gave her space. Helga was good about fussing over her, giving her soup and fluffing up her pillow.

I think Helga figured out what bothered Helen. She held her in her arms one afternoon, rocking and singing a lullaby to her. Helen began to sob on her shoulder. I stood like a stranger in the doorway.

I was the enemy. After all, I hadn't wanted the second baby. Whether an act of nature or a doctor had seen to my little problem didn't matter. I was relieved but Helen had lost another dream. How could I comfort her when I was so secretly glad? Yet I was strangely grateful to Helga for doing what I could not. Mingled with this gratitude was a terrible jealousy.

I reasoned with myself that Helga was helping us all get through this awful period, but seeing anyone, especially this fat old cow holding my Helen enraged me.

Helen was so tiny and delicate against her fat, big-boned arms. It was almost obscene. I could not get the image of Helga and Helen out of my mind, even in sleep.

I dreamed of Helga's huge frame suffocating me. Even as she smiled and comforted Helen and me, she placed a pillow over my face. I awoke to find the bed empty. Helen seemed much better. She was making breakfast with Helga. Sara sat in her high chair slopping chocolate pudding over her tray.

Domestic bliss seemed restored. Helga nudged Helen, who presented me with hot German chocolate cake for breakfast.

Perhaps it was a small price to allow Helga this influence over Helen.

Chapter 20

I GUESS I REALLY WAS relieved that Helga had returned. Less time alone with Sara was better for us both. Sometimes when Sara wouldn't stop crying, (her cry was so piercing), I would close the door to her room and go into the basement. She was in her crib and safe.

An hour later I might return to find her cooing and entertaining herself. At other times she might still be crying.

I found if I rocked her and hit the small of her back with the heel of my hand, she would calm more quickly. It was a firm, repetitive hit. Her back would redden but rarely bruise. I think it was like acupressure. It seemed to block her other discomfort by its firm insistence.

I tried mixing some herbs and Coleman's mustard and putting this small paste on the small of her back with gauze.

This worked too, but left a rashy mark which Helen fussed about.

I also found mixing a little rum into her formula calmed her. But I got worried when one afternoon she nearly choked on her vomit in the crib, so I stopped this practice.

Soon, even with Helga's return, the two afternoons with Sara were too much. Her crying pierced my senses. I would develop blinding migraines. I would retreat for periods from Sara but she was at an age where she needed time to exercise and be outside of her crib. We set up a playpen in the living room, but this was still not enough.

I suggested to Helen again that we move to the city and sell the house. Finally, she agreed that Helga could return to us full-time. This meant my time with Sara was limited to two hours per day, sometimes less. Mostly I could handle this. I loved giving her a bath and dressing her in her nightclothes. She let me sponge bathe her and was cooperative about daddy getting her nice and clean.

She would snuggle up to me for a special music tape every night. I would read the same litany of stories for her each night. She loved one about a fire engine that went "woo woo" for pages. She said "woo woo" with me. I had to repeat this story sometimes two or three times. Usually Helen would arrive about then. Most nights Helga prepared supper for us. Occasionally I would.

Sara began toilet training around this time. I would sit at the base of the toilet and make games with a little stuffed animal falling off the toilet paper roll to detain her sitting on the toilet. When she did do something, I would pretend to faint on the bathroom floor. Usually Helen would take over and put her to bed. We would eat and three nights per week, I would head out to my night editing job. Despite my intimate fantasies, I succeeded in leaving little Sara alone physically, although occasionally I would be aroused by bathing her. I never again allowed myself the taboo games you might suspect I wanted. I was content to see her naked, to touch her in the bath, and linger a moment too long. Instead I stored these memories for intimate moments with Helen. With Helga as my buffer, I was saved from my worst self.

Chapter 21

WHEN NEXT WE WENT TO church, the pastor got on my nerves.

He got off the pulpit and began pacing up and down the aisle, looking right at me.

"Adultery, fornication, men with men. Where are family values? Where are old-fashioned values? Where are the fathers? Where are the heads of their households? Are they greeted as kings or doormats? Without the man as logical king of his household, all other values break down. Women become disrespectful of their men. The value of their work in the home is denigrated."

The absolute end was his stirring words: "Let us fall on our knees before our Father and recite the words He taught us!"

As he began, "Our Father, who art in Heaven . . ., " I began to involuntarily shake. A flashback of my father touching me in the basement in the dark, my limbs covered in pink lotion. Pox scratches everywhere.

How could comfort come in those words? If God is our Father, I am cursed indeed. I shoved past Helen and out the back doors seeing nothing, a roar in my ears, heat so great I tore off my shirt. I ran some distance and fell in a grassy knoll filled with yellow and lilac wildflowers.

The red light faded to dusk before I opened my eyes again. It was the rainfall which finally quenched my fire.

Disoriented, I walked some hours until a highway patrol cop stopped beside me.

"You okay?"

I nodded, not okay.

"Your wife Helen has been pretty worried. Get in, Mister, we'll drive you home."

For once I didn't argue. My tough was all worn out.

AT HOME, HELEN ran a bubble bath and led me in. She scrubbed my back and washed my hair. She tenderly kissed my eyes and stood me up to wrap me in several towels.

She applied some delicate scented oils to massage my feet. Her grip immensely strong did not hurt but caught my pain. She moved slowly, purposefully up my legs. She grabbed the knots as if pus could squeeze from my muscles.

I lay as a babbling baby accepting her touch as a transfusion.

She placed her fingers into my ears and vibrated them, then pressed the delicate tissue around them. My face grew warm. Even my fingers and their webs were carefully rubbed, so my fingerprints and all previous life seemed gone.

Then she covered me with our quilted lace comforter, a single scented candle burning beside me. I was surely embalmed and dead for I dared not move.

I lay, my eyes open, watching the shadows dance.

SHE RETURNED TO feed me soup. The aroma was novel, its spectrum so varied, so beyond my experience. I felt I must be high.

She undressed then, her body cool against me. She lay her head on my chest, as if to say, "You are still in control. I am vanquished by you alone."

It was then that I fell asleep. My brief psychosis was my escape, my cure. Helen said I slept two days.

When I got up; it was strange to see myself in the mirror. I expected someone else. I hoped for someone else.

My beard was black compared to my tinted blonde hair. I shaved quickly.

My face was thinner, more drawn, but it was still me.

I searched my body, almost expecting to find my chicken- poxed skin; almost expecting to find a different man after all Helen had done for me.

When I arose, the house was empty. Helen had left a note.

At work, Sara at Helga's.

Love, Helen.

I called work. Helen had explained my absence. I would return tomorrow.

Sitting in the recliner I had so often used to feed Sara, I felt a fear and tightening of my chest.

I could continue to pretend I was me but something had shifted again. I was in quicksand. My steps left no footprint, no trail for me to return to.

Was I becoming something better or worse?

Was I adding layers or losing layers?

When I walked, my steps seemed quieter, less solid, so I kicked a chair to see it move.

I could not stay under this roof in this condition. Again my rage was building.

Chapter 22

FOR THE FIRST TIME IN nearly twenty years, I felt a need to return to my origins: the old farm. Surely my mother was old and sick. She had no way to reach me. My name was changed. I had not turned back once. Yet in addition to the property I inherited from my foster parents, I was entitled to the lands and buildings at the farm. It was no doubt fully paid for by Dad's untimely death.

I drove over four hours to Connecticut. I arrived unannounced. A small light was burning in the kitchen and the old stove gave up smoke despite the early thaw of spring.

I knocked timidly at the door in the back. I hardly recognized the wizened old woman who greeted me. Was this tiny creature the one who had tied me to my cot so many times? Was this the person who had allowed my father's atrocities? Or had she really not seen or heard?

Her hair, pale blond, was thin and lay in childlike curls on her wrinkled skin. One eye seemed to have a cataract, just as I remembered my lovely Nubian goat. Her stature was gone. Her back curved and her left side appeared limp.

She clearly didn't recognize me.

I introduced myself cautiously as her son, without reference to the day of my departure or my father's death.

She nodded and pulled out a chair for me. The farm was idle now. She had income from a section she rented; yes it was paid for, and would be mine.

"Could I look around?" I asked.

I had to bend to enter the basement. The doorframe seemed smaller than I remembered, although I was now 6 feet, 5 inches and taller than most doorways.

I reached automatically for the cellar light to find the pull-cord still there for my hand to find. The creak of the stairs was the same.

I was unprepared for what I found below.

The room was even more primitive than I remembered. It was just a filthy mattress on the floor. Above, a solitary bulb hung, casting a glare and ominous shadows. Stacks of newspapers tied with rope were covered by tattered plaid tablecloths. These were the bed-tables of my childhood? The concrete floor was barren save one old bathmat near the mattress. The sheets, in the pattern I remembered, were still on the bed. On the concrete floor were the stains of countless crimes. The pink calamine lotion in drops, my dear hen's blood darkened by time, the broken window boarded but unfixed.

Suddenly I felt my Gertie's blood hot running through my fingers.

I gripped the wooden railing and returned to the kitchen.

My mother old and no more my master, sat quietly unaware as always of who I was or how I had hurt so long ago.

She was a defeated soul, a shell of whoever had tortured me so long ago. Had my father heaped atrocities upon her as well?

As frightened as I was, a compulsion now gripped me. I ascended to the top floor and pulled down the old attic stairs. Again, time stood still. I was simultaneously an adult and a child. I tiptoed, cautious of who I might find.

The light switch was under my fingers without my conscious thought.

There stood all as I remembered it. I fell to my knees lest I fall altogether.

A cracked mirror blackened with age stood in a corner. In it I saw myself nude and bound at the wrist, the whistle of the whip in the air. I twirled around to look behind me, only to see an attic mouse scurry home.

The suitcases were as I remembered them. I flipped through them, avoiding the pictures I remembered too well.

My fingers trembled as I unfolded the old photograph I had found at last. So it was all true.

In the suitcase I found the other old photo of the young boy.

The picture was out of focus. I feared I was fainting or becoming psychotic. But it was only the drops falling on the picture that told me my vision was blurred by my tears

After some time I crawled to the stairs and slowly descended backwards to my mother.

Not covering the nudity, I showed my mother the face of the boy. She gasped and covered her mouth. She made the sign of the cross and backed away from me.

Finally, the words I spoke surprised me.

"Is this me, mother?" I asked.

Her face paled, her one blind eye tearing. She just kept crossing herself.

I screamed, "Is this me?"

She fell to her knees on the floor clutching at her chest.

"Witch!" I screamed. "Redeem yourself with God! Is this me?" I repeated, shaking violently now.

"I never knew," she stammered.

"Never knew?" I was incredulous with grief and rage.

Her face became red, then blue. She clutched at her chest and fell over.

How dare she dodge me with death?

I slapped her and shook her, but she was beyond my reach now.

I knelt over her, crying and shaking her until I finally fell upon her in exhaustion.

The morning sun awoke me to find my dead mother next to me, the old photo still in my hands.

The oven still smoldered as I placed each picture into it. Then I dragged her closer to it and stoked up the flame with the old leather bellows nearby.

Her dress of cotton was easily moved near the flame. I watched in disbelief as she began to catch fire and turned my back forever.

Outside I waited until I saw the entire house ablaze before driving away.

It would be easy to claim my estate.

I would write to the county clerk to inquire about her well-being in a few weeks.

Chapter 23

HOW COULD I BRING TOGETHER the subtle changes which had converged on me from Helen?

Thinking back, I could not.

As I sat in the basement writing, I could hear Helen upstairs. Sara was cruising from chair to chair. She had just begun walking, supported by our furniture.

I called out but Helen did not answer. There was a dishonesty to my situation. I was locked in the basement and she acted as if everything was normal.

Helen would never do this if she knew the flashbacks I was having, the terror I felt. Cockroaches seemed to crawl over my skin. At times, I saw my mom, my dad, and my lovely hen. The boiler light seemed to be the winking eye of the 'gloved wonder' at the State Hospital.

When I first landed in the basement, I screamed, but no one came.

Desolate woods prevented anyone from hearing me.

Helen will relent and set me free. She will even forgive me when she sees my brown roots grown out and my blue contact lenses gone, I reassured myself.

She will find me equally handsome, when she sees I have been deceiving her about my appearance.

I fully expected her to accept my charade.

She will redeem me, I thought. *The recent horrors will fade even as, Fluffy's limp body became merely a memory. She is a war veteran even as I am. She overreacted. Nothing more.*

I looked back on my behavior.

How easily she could have misinterpreted my examination of Sara, my curiosity.

I had Sara seated near the sink on the counter.

As you know, I have a quasi-scientific background. I delved into medical learning since boyhood. I am self-taught about many things. Frankly, most doctors are less adventurous or knowledgeable than myself, but I have chosen not to make science my career, merely a hobby.

There is a rigidity in our culture about roles. I could have been a shaman or a medicine man in another culture. This self-acquired knowledge would be respected, not feared.

Few pediatricians know how to manage a colicky or irritable baby, or for that matter, a hyperactive child. Doctors think that giving stimulants like Dexetrine and blood pressure pills to kids will calm them. They think they are civilized.

How is what they do less of an experiment than what I tried that day?

How could I end up in the basement in such a plight? You wonder why I'm here?

Soon, but first you must know what I endured.

My status resembled a hung man. As if suspended from a noose, I looked connected and whole from a distance. But I felt as if my head was separated from my body. So I was split.

Drinking seemed to have changed my thinking. I could feel its weird web around me. So close and suffocating was this web, yet there was no discernible pattern for me to follow.

My body seemed to break from my mind to work alone. Looking in the mirror down there, I saw a face which could not be my own.

Eight days had passed. I could not recognize myself. My hair was no longer blonde but dark primarily. A dirty, unshaven face was almost black with stubble. One blue contact lens was out. One blue eye lens was focused; the other brown one, unfocused.

So I did seem to be splitting, not only from my body but from half of myself. One half was disguised; the other half was my true appearance.

I had been reduced to an animal in my toilet habits. I used the unsettled earth of the root cellar as a litter box, these eight days.

Did I mind the loss of my dignity or mind? Not at all. For Helen I could suffer a universe of grief. She alone is my Christ, my Redeemer.

Of her love, I had no doubt, nor of her confusion.

Did I mention Sara's colic or her constant pitiful crying? Why did all this finally happen?

I became convinced that I could remedy Sara's illness non-traditionally.

I had perched Sara on the counter top near the sink. I had filled it halfway with water and ice cubes to cool her hot, perspired brow, to change her focus.

Helga came back to work for us. I mentioned that, didn't I?

Helen, therefore, was free again to go to work in the city. I was with Sara two hours a day.

Sara now could stand and pull herself around the house holding the furniture. She rarely crawled nor do I remember a moment she didn't try on my legs or Helen's to pull to a standing position.

Already she had said, "Daddy," "Mommy," "Bottle." Helga was simply "Gell."

But there were the times she would drink insatiably, her belly swollen tightly out, and she would cry to drink more. She was filled with gas and too much juice. I started diluting the milk and juice bottles before Helga returned to work.

We didn't want a fat baby. This way she could drink her fill of flavored water but not get fat.

Helga said she looked bony and took over all the feeding. She insisted she could return to work full-time with Sara and "free" me from worry.

Sara began solid baby food shortly after.

But still she was bloated and uncomfortable. The pediatrician told Helen to draw her knees up to her belly and press down on her abdomen to pump out the gas from her.

That day, I tried this first. I could hear some gas escape from her.

It was then Helen entered the kitchen early from work. Sara's legs were drawn up and apart. The sink was filled with ice cubes and I was about to plunge her only briefly into the cooling bath. Helga had gone home only an hour before.

How convenient of Helen to arrive home early this day.

She rushed toward me and grabbed Sara, who howled even more. Her winged arm hung limply.

"It's cold in here!" she shrieked. "What's with this ice bath? It's freezing winter!"

Then calm again, Helen placed Sara back on the counter, strapping her into her car seat and placing it on the floor.

So calmly she said, "I'll take her to the doctor. She may be sick; did you give her Tylenol?"

Again for the second time since I knew Helen, she fingered a lock of her hair and twirled it, so I knew she was calculating a plan.

"Could you turn up the heat," she asked so sweetly.

I opened the closet door and reached into my golf bag. But the rifle was gone.

Walking backwards, facing her, then responding with sober calmness and saccharine sweetness, I asked, "Helen, do you want to tell me something? Come, let me hug you."

She came in slow motion and we embraced. Her body was stiff against mine and her good hand fumbled with the door to the cellar.

"Maybe the pilot light has gone out again," she said. "Helga complained about it yesterday," she continued.

So she pulled the door open and asked could I check, "Honey?" and she never calls me "Honey."

I felt her heat and smelled her breath, all minty. Then so powerful and strong, like she'd given birth to her new self in front of me, she pushed me backward.

I grabbed the door frame, but my old wounded fingers could not feel to grab, so plunging backward, I fell anyway.

And she so new, so small and angry, was unrecognizable in that instant.

YES, I DISCOVERED God in this basement. Or was I just scared of the basement? I hadn't eaten in how many days?

Were the small sounds and smells God reaching out to me, or was I damned? Damned forever. Without Helen, I would be damned. She was, after all, the God who redeemed me.

Ten days finally passed. I checked my face again. My hair had gone black, both contact lenses were out. My true dark nature was revealed. My teeth seemed animal, pointy.

Where was the charming self that had wooed Helen, the blonde Aryan, blue-eyed professor?

There was a drip in the basement, suddenly. My senses, now more animal, were aware of this new sound.

A rusty odor of mud and old taps. I felt along the wall, following the sound. Did a pipe burst?

Then the realization: It was a leak from above; water was trickling down the stairs from the kitchen.

Was she washing the floor?

The water, at first slow, quickly became a steady stream.

The root cellar first soaked it up. I pushed hard against the cellar door, for the first time realizing escape was possible.

Because until that moment escape was unthinkable; my angel would get tired of this game and rescue me, I had thought. Escape was therefore unnecessary. After all, we were not enemies. She was just confused, terrified of me: a reasonable response from a trapped woman.

But now unsure, I sought escape, pushing, first panicked, then enraged, against the overhead cellar door.

A double door with a tiny latch was easy to push out and open. But up until then it was not an option for me, because if I needed to escape, then Helen must be punished.

Yet if she, contrite and confused, were to release me and accept my appearance, then all would be well again. My charade would be discovered but forgiven, we could begin again on different terms.

So I crouched in the tiny crawl space of the root cellar; pushing up against the simple old door with my full height and weight.

If my imprisonment was deliberate, the water was not. A pipe had burst above, and Helen was not at home. She could not know I was in danger.

Yet where was Helga? Where was Sara? Had they seen the burst pipe and run to get help? Was Sara away in Helga's house and me alone below?

My father crouched in my mind laughing, his trousers open, his naked, fleshy part jutted out at me. He winked and raised his finger to his lips.

I screamed the scream of death, pushing harder to escape. He was clutching me by the neck, forcing me to do unspeakable things.

And the water rushing, swirling around me mixed with the vile wet aroma of his hateful hurt. *I must escape now,* I thought.

I hurled myself upward, away from his ghost.

It was over. I lay with sunlight in my eyes and water seeping upward from the ground onto the new grass.

My eyes hurt and strained to realize that I had escaped my dungeon.

I crawled, weak and filled with hatred, not seeing Helen but his sneering mouth. This time one of his eyes was out of its socket and hanging on his cheek. And of course, his maimed hand lifted to hurt me.

I rush to the back door and the kitchen; water an inch at least, cascaded down the basement steps through the margin between the door. I rushed to its source: the sink faucet left on. Perhaps on purpose?

Chapter 24

ONCE HAVING CONTROLLED THE WATER, I removed my "litter box" mess from the basement.

I mopped up quickly as most had seeped out down the back door steps and cellar.

I next shaved and tinted my hair. Luckily, I had a pair of spare blue contact lenses. Then I searched the house. I was looking for signs of Helen's straying or indications of her frame of mind; clues I might use to know what I must do.

I searched the garbage cans in the bedroom and bathroom. I went through her coat and jacket pockets, looking for bills, notes, tickets.

I went through her underwear drawer. Was there new lingerie?

I searched her closet for new items of clothing. Finally I requested that a print-out of all long distance phone calls be faxed to me.

Then I went through the dirty laundry hamper. I sniffed her underwear for signs of bodily fluids other than my own.

All was well. My Helen had just been overwrought and frightened when she pushed me.

Of course seeing Sara with her legs drawn open; seeing the ice bath must have confused her. She panicked, nothing more.

Order could be restored with careful explanations. I went to the barber for a hair trim.

I picked up a bottle of champagne and a tiny diamond ring and had it engraved "forever." I then prepared a lasagna. I put some sausage on one end. Helen's favorite. I laced the lasagna with Valium only where I had placed the sausage, a small two by two inch piece.

I brewed some tea and added a trace of Mellaril and heaped in honey.

I would relax her initially, enough to allow my re-entry and gradually increase her state of hypnotic suggestibility with the laced lasagna, finally the champagne.

I even got a new coverlet for the bed. Wide, pink with matching satin sheets.

For Sara I simply added the usual Benadryl to her spout cup of juice. If she didn't drink this, her chocolate pudding was also mixed with it.

Sara would not disturb us tonight.

Then I checked my golf bag. The rifle was still there.

Helen hadn't found it after all. I had just not reached deeply enough into it when I last looked.

As for the basement, my mirrored workout area was still intact. I exercised strenuously for two hours. My muscles were pumped.

I still hadn't eaten. Nor did I feel weak from my ordeal. Adrenaline coursed through my veins. In the mirrors I surveyed my nude body. I was more mean and lean than ever. I was pumped up for action.

I was hard and erect as I exercised. I loved myself at different angles in the mirror. I set up my examination table for Helen.

Finally, I showered again. Then I turned off all the lights and waited. Helen returned at eight o'clock, Sara in tow. When she flicked on the lights, she gasped.

"You're back." Her eyes darted back and forth.

She placed Sara in her high chair. I walked over to Sara and held her in my left arm, my right arm beckoning Helen to me.

"Come, let's have a little reunion," I said cheerfully.

She looked anything but cheerful, but slowly she came towards me. What else could she do? I had Sara.

We ate in silence. Helen sat primly, her hands folded in her lap.

Sara said "Daddy do do, Daddy do do," and giggled. She drank half her juice and smeared her chocolate pudding.

Helen picked at her lasagna. I fed her spoonfuls as if she was an infant.

"Here's one for Auntie and Uncle," I cooed.

"Open up, here comes the airplane."

She didn't chew. She just swallowed.

I lifted the honeyed tea to her lips. Her last three spoonfuls she held in her cheeks like a chipmunk.

The tea forced her to swallow.

Despite a cool frost in the air, Helen was wearing a thin, yellow cotton dress; spaghetti straps sat on her bony collar stiffly from starch.

Her skin, translucent, revealed a rapidly pulsing carotid artery. Her chest ribs showed. The left corner of her mouth trembled, but she did not cry. Her face was hollowed and her high cheek bones more revealed. Her eyes larger than I remembered were sunk deep into much darkened sockets which added to her chipmunk expression. So pitiful, thin, and frightened was she that I burst out laughing.

Sara laughed too. She howled and stuck her hand into her chocolate pudding. Then she flung it into my face.

I sat facing Helen, my cheeks and nose covered in chocolate.

Despite herself, Helen began to laugh. The medication was working.

Sara, pleased with her success, threw yet another dollop of pudding at me which landed in my hair.

"That's it, young lady, I laughed, scooping her up with my left arm.

I pulled Helen to her feet with my right.

Then I leaned in and lifted Helen at the waist. I carried them both upstairs amid squeals of delight from both.

In the bathroom, I drew a bubble bath and undressed both my girls.

I placed Sara on Helen's lap. Then I undressed.

Once I was in the tub, the bubbles flowed over the rim. I took Sara on my lap and leaned her back on my chest.

Then I began to wash Helen. Sara was straddling my lap.

I carefully parted Helen, acting clinically, efficiently, but mindful of my effect as she sighed and leaned her head back.

I washed my face and hair quickly. I then lifted Sara out while remaining hidden under the soapy water. I used Sara's terry cloth robe to dry her. I then took my towel and draped it as I stood.

I carried Sara to her bed and wound her musical mobile. Her night light carousel twirled around its mirrored column.

When I returned, Helen was still leaning back. I lifted her and carried her wet into our bedroom. Helen was groggy. The ring and champagne could wait until morning.

No one could know the tenderness and love I felt for her.

I arranged her on the bed and carefully brushed out her long, red hair, spreading it out on the satin pillow.

I put my finger into her mouth. She did not resist. Then deeper, she sighed, then moaned. For a second, her brow flickered and her mouth trembled. Then she was mine again.

They both were.

Chapter 25

FOR THE FIRST TIME I found myself wondering what Helen's childhood had been. Her silence was a clue. Had it been similar to my own? Had her cold facts combined to create a submissive, too-tender girl? Was I a familiar echo of her childhood? I hoped not.

I did not wish her submission to me to be tainted by the shadow of the past. No nightmare figure could loom bigger than me or compete for her consciousness. The thought that she could yield to me only from the negative habit of a sordid childhood had never occurred to me. So chilled was I by this that all plans for her night with me faded.

I lay in the darkness next to her but could not bring myself to touch her. That night, sleep was a mixture of sudden fitful jolts and cold sweat. During the night I awoke and showered. I made the water as hot as I could bear.

I went to the kitchen and got bleach. I mixed a little on a sponge with dish detergent and lathered myself head to toe. Even my face and ears. Once finished, I repeated it again. I drew a hot bath and filled it with Helen's strawberry bath oil and soaked.

My eyes remained open and alert, expecting her very past to grab me as well. It was some time before I decided to open the champagne. I had told myself I wouldn't drink, but I reasoned champagne was not hard liquor. I tried to wake Helen but she was too groggy.

Finally, I took a half a Valium and slipped it under her tongue and swallowed the rest myself with champagne. The effect was minimal, but imaginings of her competitive past slipped away at least.

I was still geared up. I went downstairs and flooded the basement with light. I methodically repeated my exercise one hundred times, turning and twisting to see myself. Finally, I lay down on the examination table in front of my mirrors.

I preoccupied myself with details of my own anatomy, which I had not previously thought about. Wondering to what extent I had been stretched and examined as a child.

Then I got up again and danced slowly nude to my radio.

When I went upstairs, I was more myself.

Daylight would soon overtake us. Helga would soon enter our little separate world.

I carried Helen downstairs to the basement. I set her up naked in front of the mirrors. When I tried to put her feet into the stirrups of the examination table, she stiffened slightly. Despite the sedation, she remained stiff each time I tried to place her feet.

I took her pulse and found it rapid, rather than slow, as it should have been. Some balance was shifting again. My anger surfaced.

I carried Helen upstairs and again placed her on our bed. Methodically, my rage taking over, I arranged her body again on the bed. I shaved her and placed Josie's leather belt on her.

Then, because I knew what I could do in that instance, I fled.

I opened the refrigerator and ate all the chocolate chip ice cream. I hadn't eaten in days. I was more susceptible to ghosts and anger than usual. I drank out all the milk from the container. Then I went back upstairs.

She was lovely. Saliva ran out the side of her mouth, wetting the pillow. Her hair, now dry, was in ringlets about her face.

I sat opposite her, then deliberately twisted her ankle. I don't think I planned it. It just happened. The thought of temporarily disabling her was a thought.

Later, I removed the belt and hid it in the golf bag.

Although I think I experimented I do not remember.

When I awoke, it was to Sara's babbling and the doorbell. I was on top of Helen, her body face down. I took Sara down and opened the door.

Helga took Sara silently and grunted when she entered.

I went upstairs without comment. I dressed Helen in her nightgown and lay next to her.

We drifted off until evening. Helga rapped sharply on the door at seven.

"I'm leaving, Sara has eaten."

"Great," I said, trying to sound casual.

I put Sara to bed after her little bedtime ritual.

Helen was still sleeping, so I awoke her. She was sluggish but relaxed. I helped her to the bathroom. She limped a little, but could bear her own weight to get up from the toilet.

The pain woke her further. In the bedroom I knelt and asked her if she was hungry. She reached for her ankle and massaged it, puzzled. It was slightly swollen and a little discolored.

"No more champagne for you, young lady," I said, pointing to the bottle. "I think you may have twisted your ankle," I said, examining it.

She seemed to accept that.

I helped her downstairs and got out the remaining lasagna. We ate in peace.

Helen recovered after a month or so, no wiser about how she hurt her ankle. She never mentioned that I had shaved her.

You know, in the world of possibilities and impossibilities, we seemed to drift back into our previous patterns.

It was as if I had never been locked in the basement.

I could easily forgive Helen this lapse.

She forgave everything in me.

Chapter 26

TO NURTURE HELEN AND RESTORE our balance more, I got another dog for her. I reasoned she had lost her second dream child. I came into the house with the little pup under my coat. I let Sara see it first. She was delighted. We called it Puffy. I even brought a little bottle to feed it. It was a hit. It was unique. One eye was brown, the other blue. Even I found it appealing.

In the glow of evening, with only the Tiffany lamp on, Helen held her little bundle and fed it the bottle. In my own mind, I made a vow never to harm this dog.

I also gave her space and I tolerated it in our bed. When she was asleep, I placed it into a little plaid and wicker bed on the floor.

We enrolled Sara in a half-day program of "gymnastics/ nursery" three mornings a week. Helga took her and picked her up.

I did call the county clerk for Fairfield, Connecticut. He explained that my mother had passed and expressed sympathy. The matter of papers and deeds could be handled in a month or so. No funeral arrangements needed to be made due to the "thoroughness" of the fire's heat. However, a memorial "could be arranged."

I explained that we would do this closer to my current home and thanked him.

A few weeks later, I officially took ownership of my parents' farm. The couple who rented could continue at their leisure. A local real estate broker would collect rents and hold them for me.

Chapter 27

ABOUT TWO MONTHS PASSED TRANQUILLY, then in the middle of the night I smelled smoke. The detector went off soon after. I swept Helen under one arm and Sara under the other. I picked up Puffy by his long hair and dumped him under my pajama top, then ran downstairs. The fire was in the heating vent. I put Sara and Helen down on the lawn and ran back. By the time I came back, the flames were licking the carpet and drapes. I threw a bucket into the kitchen sink as I ran in. I yanked the curtains down and began stomping them and the carpet. Then I ran back to get the bucket of water. The fumes were awful.

Sometime during all this Helen crept back and called the fire department. The engines pulled up within minutes. You can imagine my terror when I returned to the outdoors and saw Sara crying but no Helen.

I rushed back to the house; by now visibility was limited.

"Helen," I screamed between coughing.

The firemen pushed me out and slammed the door.

I began pounding. "Helen, my Helen's in there!"

Finally, I went over to a window and threw a rock in. Big mistake; this spread the fire more quickly. From the window, I could see Helen near the phone table on the floor.

I climbed into the living room. The smoke choked me. I had to feel my way, all the while I was screaming her name.

I lifted her and crouched down low to shuffle back to the window. When I lowered her to the ground, she was sooty. Her lashes and brows were gone and some of her hair. Her normally pale face was beet red from the heat of the fire. Her flimsy nylon nightgown was melted onto her left breast.

Fortunately, only this burn occurred on her lovely body. I, too, lost my lashes and some hair, a small price to pay to save my little family.

Despite his constant "yapping," I had forgotten to remove Puffy from my pajama top.

He, too, suffered smoke inhalation.

In retrospect, I think what woke me was Puffy's yapping. The smoke detectors failed to beep until it was too far gone to stop. Puffy was by my side of the bed, barking on his hind legs. Frankly, if he hadn't been there, I would have forgotten him.

My attitude toward him was changed. Really. You know, he saved us all, I think. No cheap sentimentality, just fact.

SARA SEEMED NONE the worse for the experience, although she missed Helen, who was treated for burns. Her face gradually peeled but there would be no scarring. She had breathed in less smoke because she was on the floor and smoke rises. The doctors thought perhaps a molten ember from the drapes blew onto her when the window was broken.

The two-inch patch on her left breast began to heal without a graft. They called it a second-degree burn. She wore a bandage on the area and went frequently for follow up to avoid infection. It was a little more serious than its size due to its location.

Some may say I am redeemable because I cared for my little family. I say it is self-survival. After all, without them I am a living dead, aren't I? Besides, they are mine. They belong to me, *not* God.

I don't subscribe to the notion that God snatches his little angels back to protect them from greater suffering or some other crap. Face it: if there is a God, why didn't God save me?

I figure God is busy with basic maintenance or set everything going and has a non-interference policy. I will admit that my Helen gives me pause to reflect on the beauty of all that is pure and light.

So she is my God on earth, isn't she?

On the day she ceases, "the veil between Heaven and earth will be torn," for on that day all life will end.

If there is a right hand of God, I do not care. I wish only to be on the right hand of Helen for eternity. Is that possible?

I went to a shrink again. Naturally I had to do this to get sedatives for my Helen but I did discuss my own alcohol "recovery" process.

I didn't tell my innermost thoughts. I just wanted to see if I could get a handle on my unpredictable rages. I didn't tell anything factual. I whitewashed my stories. I'd say I smashed a lamp down, that kind of thing. The psychiatrist was about fifty, looked impish, short, dowdy. I told her, "I don't want to drag up my past, I'm dealing in the here and now."

I didn't expect to change. My exploratory nature is who I am. Maybe I wanted greater control for my sake and Helen's. That's it.

Very little matters when you're thinking in black and white. There is either absence or line. There is a refinement, a clarity, no distraction of color or hue. My life with Helen is this. I work; I make love. I do not possess an imagination. My imagination becomes an action; witness Josie. What could I imagine which I have not done? What could I wonder that I haven't tried? My needs, my satisfactions are simple. Only when I shock myself must I worry?

No?

So the ankle thing shocked me. I wanted my Helen to thrive and stay my captive bird. If this required a dog, a child, so be it.

If some restraint is necessary in her or myself, I am willing.

But do not think I am a loser or a small person. I am a high roller. I confine myself to games I know and parlors where I can win. I am a high roller in my castle now and unlike a compulsive gambler I choose my games and partners.

Oh, some impulsivity may appear to decrease my odds. But you are wrong. Josie was an accident, no more. A well calculated whim perhaps. Helen was perfectly planned.

She does not think ahead. She talks about the future only. But all of her being is in the present with me.

I can calibrate my breathing , my pace to her. I can plant a seed in thought and deed. She possesses it as her own.

One night she sat on the new porch. I built it with my own hands. The two-seater swing faced outward to the stars and moon, precisely where the trees dip and the pond frogs jump. The wind inclines to the right most nights and in summer the bamboos lean in. The porch awning I added can be rolled down to block sun or give privacy.

I love to see my Helen in all lights from early morning to moonlight. So I built an exquisite porch. I painted it white and stenciled a tiny moon at each corner with stars in black.

Helen could freely sit in her nightgown to swing.

I led her into the house with her eyes covered the day I completed it. With her eyes still closed, I brought her out and I sat her on the swing, a tiny plate of scallops in wine on the side table. A bucket of chilled champagne was nearby.

I knelt at her feet and guided her to remove my shirt, sweaty from work. I removed my socks and shoes and sat next to her.

I pushed off her sandals with my toes and pried open the cork of the bottle.

Her little red paisley cotton dress had a satin bow at the throat. I untied it and gently I folded up the hem. She swooned and looked back at the house. She began to say "Sara," but I put my finger up to her lips. She looked at the scallops and seemed to relax.

I fed her one. She didn't even chew it. Then she noticed the silk pink scarves at each corner of the swing. Her eyes were desperately wide.

I poured the champagne for each of us. We crossed glasses, sipping from each other's. Just a sip for me, of course. No one can know this dance as I do. She barely breathed. I took her waist to guide her up to dance. One hand on her waist, the other sipping her glass of champagne; she sipping mine. I poured her more until the scallops and drink were gone. I didn't wait for her to become silently passive from sedative or drink.

I took hold of her consciousness with my eyes and dropped the dress to her ankles. I wanted to see her bend to my will first.

I lowered the porch awning and kissed her into the chair. My hand never left her. She knew what I wanted. I continued to be gentle but willed her to my needs by waiting and bringing my hips close to her face.

Night was falling. No light within the house illuminated us, only the moon. She seemed reassured by nightfall.

As she allowed me my fantasy, she grew drowsy. The silk scarves couldn't hurt her. They merely instructed her on where to remain once I arranged her.

I pushed her as if she was a baby in her cradle enjoying the privilege that my mastery allowed.

Chapter 28

AS I HAVE MENTIONED, SARA was a colicky baby. With the onset of language, the terrible "two's" replaced her colic.

She was still a lovely child. Since she was rarely with me for more than an hour or two at most, I could be patient with her tantrums. I would ignore her or walk away.

I had seemed to become more irritable myself, after all. My usual outlets for tension were latent. For over three months I had left Helen alone. Nor had I sought interest outside our home. I was a changed man, not on best behavior, but altered.

I dreaded another effort with Helen, which might be frustrating. She had been unable to walk properly for over a month from the last time I had frightened myself by my direct, unexpected rage and the twisting of her ankle. I stopped all alcohol again and began attending A.A. meetings twice a week. I was being practical. I needed to stay sober to avoid my own terrible tantrums.

Sara had developed into quite a young lady at two and a half years. She wore her little pierced earrings and gold cross at all times. The gold against her skin highlighted her delicate features.

Her eyes, though quite dark, had flecks of hazel. Her face was flawless and bore a permanent question mark. She seemed always puzzled about her surroundings, though also a wise sage in a child's body. Her favorite toy was a plastic baby doll with blue eyes and frizzy blonde hair. The blonde doll's fairness accentuated Sara's exotic features. Her hair was shiny and pin straight. Her eyes were decidedly Asian looking. Like many Asian children, she seemed miniature in size, but fully developed and in proportion. Her skin also had a gold cast as if she was in the sun. Since I am dark in reality I have no doubt she is mine. She even walks like me; she favors her right side. When she walks, she tilts to the right and often trails the right wall to turn corners. I too trail the wall as I turn a corner.

If I ever implied I was sexually turned on by Sara, I correct that notion now. For one thing, I have been disinterested for several months, as I have mentioned. Maybe I'm afraid Helen will get pregnant again, who knows? But I have no interest in Sara in that way.

To test this, several times I washed her, with myself naked except for a towel. Nothing happened. I placed her on her blanket undressed, with the house properly heated, of course, and took videos of her chattering and playing with her blonde baby. The adjustable lens allows her to have utter privacy for her play while I can look closely at her development from afar. Even when she sleeps I do this. Trust me when I say that nothing happens. I am merely a spectator, a journalist chronicling her growth in detail.

When she is with me, nothing happens. Later, when I have viewed my videos, I have tried unsuccessfully to arouse myself, which is how I know she is safe from me.

Perhaps my lack of tension outlets also is increasing my irritability. At A.A., they suggest drinking coffee or a lot of orange juice. I'm taking vitamin supplements as well. When I work out strenuously, it helps.

Recently, when Sara was sick, I took a rectal reading of her temperature. Helen caught me and she was livid. She yanked Sara away and placed the thermometer under Sara's armpit instead. I didn't know you could do this. It was just plain stupidity. No foul play was intended. She, of course, was able to see that when I explained it.

I pulled her chair into a corner with Sara and grabbed Sara back. Then I lifted Sara high into the air.

"Suppose I drop her now?" I asked Helen. "Do you think I would deliberately hurt our child?" I asked. I asked her slowly like she was a dumb child herself.

Then I raised Sara again and placed my hand on her naked bottom.

"Don't you realize I could do worse?" I said. "Do you think I would do such a thing in front of you, Helen?"

By this time I was screaming. Sara started to cry. Since she was already sick, I gave her back to Helen. What was the point of over-instructing Helen on the obvious?

Helen was very quiet. Her eyes were wide like a doe in front of a truck at night. She knew too well the tone of my voice.

As I hurriedly put on my coat, she cradled Sara on her lap in a dazed, almost vacant way. She kept repeating, "Mommy knows what to do . . . Mommy knows what to do . . .," in a monotone, to herself. I left the house. I drove around awhile and eventually went to an A.A. meeting.

By the time it was over, I was calmer. I ate a huge, family-size bag of candy during the meeting. Then I went for ice cream.

When I got home, the house was quiet. The aroma of apple popovers was in the air. My mother used to make popovers . . . Nice try, Helen! Just smelling them was nauseating.

Maybe all the junk I ate kicked in. I opened the windows. Then I quietly shredded the popovers into the toilet.

When I caught her watching me in the bathroom mirror, I startled. I felt like a child throwing away his dinner. This again flared my rage, but I artfully controlled it. I was humiliated somehow that she was spying on me.

"I know you meant well," I continued.

"Oh, I meant to say so much," she said. "I thought, I meant to please you," she stammered.

This was the right thing to say to me. It was as if I was reborn or my heart had been pried open, but the lock undamaged.

She was in a velvet green bra and night shorts. Talcum clung to her toe tops. A delicate aroma which was new arose from her: a mixture of almonds and baby powder. She had prepared herself for me.

No more the child bride but more the artful seducer.

Her hair hung long and full and she looked down as if shy. Oh my dear Helen.

It was then I realized she was wearing the gold bangle bracelets and Josie's tiny gold ring on her toe.

She took my hand but didn't direct me. She awaited my direction. I pivoted her to the toilet seat, then pulled her head and neck back sharply. No resistance. Her jaw was slack. Her lips now parted and were suddenly bloodless.

Her eyes looked set on a target on the ceiling. They didn't close. I yanked harder. She was on the floor instantly. No sound escaped from her lips. No rebellion was visible, but for the first time in our relationship, she purposefully looked into my eyes.

Not a quick, furtive glance, but a studied and focused look. She was not there as I knew her for an instant. Then it was gone.

She closed her eyes and went limp. Perhaps she fainted. Or did she surrender? I stopped caring.

I closed the bathroom door and locked it. I hooked the bangles together on each wrist and placed her in the bathtub. hooking them also over the faucets. Then I sat on the toilet and watched her, "cuffed" to the tub.

I studied my Helen.

Was she pretending to comply? She was not sedated. She was limp and pliant. An hour must have passed before I shaved and disrobed. I filled the tub partially and washed as I gazed at her.

When I was ready, I lifted her, casting aside the gold bracelets. On the bathroom rug, her head against the toilet base, I mounted her. This alone released my months of pent-up sexuality.

I lay on top of her, grateful, and cried for the first time in my adult life.

TWO NIGHTS LATER Helen voluntarily came to the swing. She held Sara in her lap with her winged arm and used the other to grasp the swing.

She was in her robe and Sara in her pajamas. The heat of summer was coming fast. She abandoned her robe and quickly removed Sara's pajamas. It was muggy and hot even as the sun went down.

I watched them both from my white wicker rocker. The brilliant floral print of the swing pillows accentuated their fiery hair.

I put my hand on Helen's thigh and pushed them back and forth. Puffy came out too, so I pulled him up.

Helen had almost entirely healed. A scar the size of a quarter remained. The fire damage was paid for by our insurance and in fact we turned a little profit. Enough to refurbish the house and then some.

The scar had the effect of a tiny tattoo. It merely looked seductive on her milky torso.

I pushed them and watched as Sara and Helen grew sleepy. I could feel Helen's warmth increase and could smell the musky fragrance that heat and seduction emitted. I liked touching Helen here with Sara passively involved, but I knew not to take it too far, at least initially.

I packed little Sara up to bed and took Puffy inside.

When I returned Helen had curled into a fetal position on the swing.

I was content to reach under her nightgown and continue to gently touch her. Here in the heat of the porch, the privacy was balanced by the public format. The pond and trees, the twinkling of the highway far ahead opened our domestic scene to a reverse voyeurism.

Although I knew we were not watched, the "public" outdoor location pleased me. I didn't care if in fact anyone did choose to watch for all they would see was what they could never have.

It was easy to add the scarves as a bond but why bother? Except that it pleased me to do so. I didn't even have to touch her to simply remain aroused by her beauty and vulnerability.

By this time in our lives together, I really no longer needed to continue working. I had set up both properties to be income—producing, but I knew that time on my hands was unsafe for Helen and Sara. I needed an outlet for my energies and an excuse for disappearances. Work in the city gave me both.

I rocked and observed Helen for over an hour, occasionally easing her clothing further up. When I was ready I partially mounted her.

I enjoyed my standing position over her body.

Chapter 29

WE NEVER HAD DISCUSSED MY basement imprisonment. Nor did I question her about the water which leaked that day. It was thankfully a convenient trick of ours that we erased what was unpleasant from our collective memory.

Similarly the fire was never discussed.

I often did wonder to what extent she knew how I possessed her. Did she have an inkling of the many facets of my love for her? Would she embrace them in consciousness as she must when sedated?

She still resisted the basement and my little games before the mirrors. Even sedated some part of her would react with rigidity. So I abandoned this part of our life together. The porch was a new diversion for me.

As was my custom I checked Helen's pockets and wallet every night. For the first time in our relationship I found a picture of another man.

It was an old picture worn away with handling and time. The edges were rounded and the oil from her fingertips had softened them. It had the unmistakable fragrance of Helen and time.

The young man I faced was a handsome teenager maybe frozen in time some twenty years before. He resembled me greatly, even to the blonde hair and blue eyes. Mine of course were fake. His were not.

My rage was enormous. Had this picture only recently surfaced or was it merely my first success at finding it?

It was difficult to contain myself. We ate supper in silence. Rather than going to work, which was my custom, I was tempted to stay home and question Helen. Finally, I decided that a full confrontation was dangerous. I replaced the photo and prepared for work.

I think Helen knew I was upset but she accepted this as outside of her control. She made a flutter of getting Sara ready for bed and fussed over a homemade sorbet she had made with strawberries.

Sara was in a nursery education play-group for parents. Helen tried to engage me to go with them.

When I arrived at work I could barely focus.

I found a midnight A.A. meeting and went. Finally, for the first time I spoke.

I blurted out, "I found another man's picture in my wife's wallet."

No one responded. They looked concerned and waited. My mouth was twitching. I tried drinking coffee but sipping from the container made it worse.

"It was very old," I finally continued.

"Maybe an old boyfriend or a relative," someone volunteered.

"What were you doing in her wallet?" someone else asked.

Now I regretted speaking. All eyes were pinned on me.

"Let go of it," someone mumbled.

"How can I?" my tone fairly attacked the speaker.

"Give it to God," someone else said.

"Oh, the God who ain't there for me?" I spat out.

"The God who gave you Helen," an elderly man answered.

I began to cry. Not sadness but tears of frustration and rage. The group formed a circle closer to me and the elderly man tentatively lay his hand on my shoulder. I exploded, pushing his hand off my shoulder and knocking over the metal folding chair I was sitting on. I could see the offensive picture in flames in my mind; the room was on the periphery of this vivid image.

When I got back to my job I was in no condition to work.

I took two of the sedatives I usually reserve for Helen. I ate a huge omelet from the take-out diner at the corner.

When I left work a little after five in the morning, my shift was not over. I couldn't concentrate so I just left.

As I walked along I became aware of a thin muscular boy in front of me. His right arm seemed longer than his left. He walked with a disjointed jiggle. He walked into the back entrance of a restaurant and asked if anyone wanted sex with him.

I saw a hand push him outward; he was rubbing the front of his pants and even rubbed against the doorframe.

His face seemed to bulge out of itself.

Spittle was on his lips and his eyes were glassy red. He looked high on drugs or drunk but mostly filled with an insane, hateful sexuality.

I took out a twenty-dollar bill, folding it lengthwise, and placed it between my teeth. His eyes missed nothing. He crossed over to my side.

He rubbed himself again and asked for a cigarette. We stopped at a newsstand where I got a pack. He swiped at my hand to grab the pack but I doled out one to him.

He had on new clothing on which included khakis and a business shirt. He was unable to properly fill them. It was as if he was fluid leaking and bubbling: unable to find his own end and the beginning of the garments.

He fell in step with me and continued to loudly taunt the air with his offer of oral sex. Finally, he dropped down to a filthy blanket below. There he had barbecued corn chips and other debris strewn including orange juice and a pint of vodka. I again pulled out the twenty. For one so gone, he saw it immediately.

He arose and began his profanities.

I said, "More if you shut up . . . ." He did.

There was sadness to this youth gone wrong. He seemed schizophrenic, so chemically altered was the substance of his being. Someone so young and tiny in stature may have arrived in the city as a runaway, perhaps molested at home and foolishly thinking that if he could just arrive in New York City he'd be all right.

He obviously earned well for what he was willing to do. Even his shoes were expensive. Yet his immediate need for his own gratification meant he didn't save. He needed to get the sex he gave. He was horny as a diseased dog in the road.

He was repulsive in every way. But his utter isolation and underlying sadness redeemed him. Perhaps I saw myself as I might have become some twenty years before.

I loved this sense of sad ruin. It was his "broken wing" of the soul. I could violate him, abuse him, beat him and he would allow it. He would feed off of this, knowing his superiority for being needed by me.

I whispered as I leaned into him, "Follow at a safe distance with your shoes on . . . quietly."

He was floridly psychotic and his lips were full and so red, as only youth can be. I saw he was fully aroused by my orders. Perhaps he was never any less than aroused. I didn't care. It was what I needed.

We arrived at my apartment. His eyes looked around briefly, almost simultaneously, he was disrobing.

"No," I said. "Stay dressed. Sit on this chair."

He sat but fairly darting out of his skin.

"Now unzip and take your penis out." I sat opposite him.

He could be covered in lice and convey every known disease, but he was smug knowing I wanted him.

I got a hefty bag and opened it in front of him.

"Take off your clothes and drop them in," I told him.

He seemed relieved to have a chance to undress. He kept licking his lips and wiping his nose with the back of his hand.

I led him to the bathroom where I donned rubber gloves.

When he was in my tub I lathered his body with delousing shampoo and covered him meticulously. Then I rinsed him. When I lathered his penis he sighed and held my hand there. I removed it quickly.

Squeaky clean, standing nude before me, he was a pygmy in size, under five feet, but pure sinewy muscle and bones. His pathetic youth and diseased metabolism stripped him of calories.

I brought him into my kitchen wrapped him in a large, fluffy white terry cloth robe. I cooked him a hamburger and made him eat it. It was sedated with Mellaril.

I led him to the bed in silence. Again he was aroused. He lay down. But I sat in a chair and watched him. Then he thought he knew what I wanted and began touching himself and moaning.

"Quiet; stop that!" I commanded.

He was now confused completely. His edge of smugness receded. He seemed almost shy.

I just stared at him for perhaps an hour. When he finally fell asleep, I was weary—weary of him and myself.

I examined his body. It was badly scarred especially his back and behind. Even his penis looked scarred. Ironically his feet were uncalloused as a youngster's often are.

In sleep he was as beautiful as a girl.

His backside had been violated repeatedly as evidenced by tearing and scars. Even his anus was scarred. A recent "gift" from an admirer had left a blister filled with pus—probably a burn.

No wonder he was gone.

I couldn't hurt him or even accidentally kill him.

I applied triple antibiotic ointment to my gloved fingers and glided them over his lacerated behind and then gently in.

He would heal better this way. How could I violate him further in this state?

He moaned. I hugged him from behind and grasped his aroused body. Although sedated he responded quickly.

We slept. In the morning I washed him lightly in front and carried him like a baby to my rocking chair. I held this tiny man/child on my lap and rocked him all day, occasionally marveling at his tiny smile which restored his innocence in my mind.

He was a victim. I could heal him.

I fed him a half-gallon of chocolate ice cream again laced with sedatives. Not to drug him, but to heal his diseased state and assist his rest.

I called Helen and made apologies for my lateness. I would be doing some overtime. Not to worry.

I had added an additional lock inside our apartment, which closed with a key. Helen could not enter if she by chance had decided to visit. I doubted she would. I think in her mind our life was fully in Monroe, New York. But I took no chances. My guest could not leave without my permission either.

By evening, he was dreamily awake. He curled up in my arms on the rocker. I think he was only about fourteen, now that I had held him in my arms. Even in his dreamy relaxed state I had only to touch him for him to become aroused. Perhaps it was age or survival instincts from the street, or his still diseased excesses. No matter.

Finally, I lay him on the bed.

I prepared myself and gently guided him into me sitting down as a woman might.

He grabbed my front but I pulled his hand away. He was to take me and satisfy himself. But I was in power. This was my choice.

He moved tenderly perhaps relieved to let his own body rest. I had protected myself by putting a condom on him.

This did not dull his sensation. His arousal was almost neurological as I have said.

He came in seconds.

I lay next to him and stroked his head, placing it on my chest. He slept again, as did I.

When I awoke he was creeping through the house looking through my bureau drawers. There was nothing to steal anyway. I watched his cunning and stealth. He thought he fooled me.

What he chose to take was pathetic. A half-empty cologne bottle, a silk pocket-handkerchief. He dropped these things into his pants pockets in the hefty bag.

Then he went through my pockets looking for money. My wallet was hidden under the mattress with my keys.

I made an obvious show of awakening. He crept back into bed and pretended to be asleep.

Street people are no match for me. I have lived on the edge. I always think the worst and plan ahead.

So he was healing nicely.

"Would you like me to get you some jeans and a new shirt?" I asked.

He shrugged. I didn't want his filthy clothes to re-contaminate him.

I made him a cheese omelet with fried potatoes and toast. His coloring was more normal, less peculiarly flushed. His eyes though glassy seemed more focused.

When I left for work that night he was in a blissful sleep.

I got him a change of clothes, underwear, socks and sneakers, even a wallet for the money I would give him.

When I returned he had made us both noodle soup from a package. He sat nude to eat with me. He accepted our arrangement. He had been locked in all day and had no doubt slept. I called Helen again and said I had some business to take care of out of town. I would be back in several days.

I kissed him passionately on the mouth and carried him to bed.

Again I was interested in games. I removed two tiny nipple clips from my pocket and attached them to each of his little nipples. They are designed to gently inflict stimulation, not damage. He lay still and trusting.

I gloved my hand, lubricated it with antibiotic ointment and glided it into him.

He sighed. I was exquisitely gentle.

I wanted to tease him but not abuse him. He smiled a knowing smile. I didn't like this so I removed the clips and my hand.

He had made me angry. I knew this was dangerous. I left the house immediately to go to an A.A. meeting. When I returned I was calm again and he was sleeping. I dressed him.

He could still walk on his own power. We walked to a teen shelter in mid-town that was for runaways. I rang the bell and left him like a bundled baby on a doorstep. Perhaps he could get help.

In his own way he had helped me.

His war-torn soul revived me. He was so fragile that in the end, I couldn't hurt him. Yet his utter powerlessness with me protected him and restored me to my better self again.

Chapter 30

I STILL HAD THE DILEMMA that Helen was concealing an old photograph of a handsome male in her wallet. My rage was the original reason I had fled our home and sought diversion in the city.

I decided my so-called therapist could help me with this. Yes, I admit it was a departure for me, but I was merely getting another perspective. I was isolated in many ways up until now.

I told her the facts only, not the rage. I did not mention my little sojourn in the city, either.

"I came to tell you I found an old photo in Helen's wallet . . ." I began.

"Really?" she responded, as if I was a child.

"Yes, really! Let's cut the Freudian crap," I exploded. Then I caught myself and regrouped.

"You're upset," she stated.

"Of course, wouldn't you be?" I shot back.

"Well who is it?" she asked.

"I don't know," I said.

"How did you find it in her wallet?" she asked.

This was tricky.

"Oh, I was getting some cash from it and saw it in there," I responded.

"Well, couldn't you ask her about it?" she ventured.

"But what if I don't like her answer or I get upset with her?" I explained.

"If you are concerned about a blow up, take a sedative or your Mellaril an hour beforehand."

"But what if I still get upset or don't like what I hear?" I continued.

"Leave the house, go to an A.A. meeting or call me. For an emergency I can be reached," she replied.

I was stunned. For one thing the medicine was for Helen—for our special games, not for me. It hadn't occurred to me that I might actually use what was prescribed for me.

I was so used to manipulating the doctor to get a prescription for Helen's sedation. I was amazed that she would inconvenience herself for me.

She passed me the box of tissues, indicating to take one. "What were you just thinking?" she asked more gently than usual.

"Why?"

She remained silent.

"What the hell," I thought. I blurted out, "That you would inconvenience yourself for me; that you think my situation is important to address . . . That I matter," I finally whispered.

Now I understood the tissues. I wiped my eyes.

"Don't you matter?" she asked matter of factly.

I saw my father holding the unfolded photo of the little boy. It was me . . . .

I saw light and felt unspeakable terror and pain. Burning, searing fire. Deep inside me.

I gasped; I couldn't breathe. I was choking.

Deep inside me.

Burning, tearing.

Blackness, hate, timeless hell and his laughter.

Squeezing my heart, tearing it out.

Giving me the boots. Finally, abandoned in the dark in the basement.

The therapist was suddenly holding me and rocking me, but I began to flail about. She was so strong and gentle, stroking my head.

I passed out. As I write this, I perspire and gasp to know it in memory. Then she was leaning over me. She was quiet.

"What?" I said.

"You passed out."

"Oh."

"I'm increasing your medication," she said. "Have you been taking it?"

"No." For no reason, I told the truth.

"What about the Valium?"

"Yes," I answered. I had been using it. Sometimes to cut the effects of alcohol withdrawal. Mostly I needed it for my recreational activities. So I had my "happy campers" cooperating . . . .

"If you are still angry . . . in a worrisome way or panicky, you just call me. We need to meet a little more often . . . just for the here and now," she added.

"We will keep in the present at all times . . . I promise," she added.

So anyway, I decided not to talk to Helen just yet. Mainly because I wasn't really ready. And frankly, what the fuck did I care about some old picture? I reasoned.

Chapter 31

I GOT CURIOUS ABOUT THE fourteen-year-old I had dropped at the teen shelter. So I called; I didn't even know his name.

"I dropped off a homeless boy of about fourteen, black hair, very thin, probably alcoholic, maybe addicted. Did he stay? Is he all right? I think he was schizophrenic . . . He was wearing new clothes."

"Sir, we cannot divulge his name or information. It is strictly confidential," was the reply.

I knew that, of course.

"He had been abused sexually, I think," I continued.

"Sir, ninety-five percent of the teen runaways we see fit that profile . . . they come into Port Authority Bus Terminal looking to change their lives; within a few days, they're pimped and addicted. It's routine . . . ."

"I didn't know. It's just, well, he seemed like such a nice, desperate kid . . . ."

I didn't add that I had planned my own games for him.

"All I can say is that he was hospitalized and is responding well. We can give him a message . . . ."

"Oh, he was in such bad shape, he wouldn't remember me. Anyway, he didn't know my name," I replied. "Will he eventually return?"

"Perhaps, or he may go into another rehabilitation program or a 'safe' house."

"Well, thank you . . . ." I hung up.

Chapter 32

TIME CHANGED FOR ME FOR awhile.

I rushed out of Helen's presence I spent less time in the house.

I did more household tasks. Rebuilding the cellar door, adding an additional room to the house and an enclosed porch area as a foul weather playroom for Sara.

I even made a wooden rocking horse for Sara. I added a yarn tail and mane plus a bell necklace. It was her favorite thing. I built a new phone table and redid the trim on the windows where the fire had charred them.

I really did put extra hours in at work. So much so that they again offered me a raise and promotion. They put me in charge of all the legal editing with an assistant, but I was able to continue working at night. The assistant was in another room and kept to himself.

I didn't like the legal briefs; they were too dry and required meticulous form. I came home at night with frequent migraines around this time.

I finally asked for another assistant and got back my fiction editing half of the time.

One brief caught my attention. It involved a child custody battle. One parent alleged the other was abusive of the three year-old girl. There had been doctor's examinations and psychiatrist interviews with the little girl. All were inconclusive according to the brief.

The father was a prominent judge and had also run for political office a few years earlier.

I became obsessed with this case. I couldn't sleep at night. I fantasized torturing the father.

I knew that you could insert your finger into little girl's vagina or anus without "damaging" her. I knew that you could fondle, rub and vicariously get your "rocks" off without leaving evidence.

I knew most of all about the mother's complicity. She had looked the other way for three years.

Now she wanted custody. I somehow wasn't upset about her.

I kept thinking of him.

I knew where the law firm was so I hung out outside there before work.

I knew him immediately from the papers.

He was tall, smug and pampered looking. His fingernails were manicured with clear polish. His loafers were made of calf skin and had gold tassels. His hair was lacquered into place and woven with a hairpiece. It was grey but had a bluish cast, a "whitening" rinse in it.

If it was possible to hate him more; his proximity inflamed me more.

Then as I gazed over my paper I realized he was gay or bisexual. I followed him for several nights once I knew where he lived.

His pattern was to frequent an Italian restaurant near his apartment. He'd get a few drinks at the bar then move to a single table for linguine, usually in clam sauce.

Then I carried out my plan.

I darkened my hair at my apartment, left out my blue lenses, and wore a hat and tight fitting white cotton pants with no underwear. I pulled a cashmere cardigan over my polo shirt. It covered my behind and crotch. I had two hundred dollar moccasin shoes on but no socks. In my shirt pocket I had put a Mickey Mouse silk handkerchief, a conversation piece.

I had on a Coach belt with a brass buckle. I shot about three hundred dollars in new clothes but combined some thrift shop pieces such as my briefcase and hat. My hat was an old felt fedora with new satin trim. It concealed my face but drew attention to me for his sake.

I got to the bar a moment or two after him. I ordered the drink I knew he usually ordered. When his came, I took it and began to sip. He interrupted me to say that it was his drink.

"You should be more careful." He was pissed.

I tipped my hat graciously and flashed my most winning smile. Then I replied in a southern accent, "Actually, it's just that I've been rushing all day. What did you order?"

He told me. I laughed. I gushed my warm cordial laugh. "I ordered the same. No wonder our confusion," I drawled. "May I at least give you mine?" I offered it just as the bartender placed it down.

He laughed in spite of himself.

I fumbled in my pockets to find my wallet.

"Oh my goodness," I said. "I rushed so much I left my wallet on my desk. Oh, could you? Would you mind watching my briefcase? I'll be right back," I said and was gone before he could say no.

After a good fifteen minutes, I returned of course to find him at supper. "Thank you." I was deferential but aristocratic. "I'm famished. I think I'll just stay here for supper. Can you recommend an entree?" I asked. Before he could speak, I said, "I can never get good linguine in clam sauce."

He laughed heartily. "Two peas in a pod we are," he said. "That's what I ordered. It's excellent here."

I surveyed the room and played my last card.

"God, I'm hot from rushing about."

I lifted the coral cashmere sweater over my head.

I stretched my trunk and arms up to accentuate my tight crotch and of course thin white cotton pants.

Then I tied it over my shoulders. Not before daubing my brow with my silk Mickey Mouse pocket-handkerchief.

He laughed again. Then I gazed around for a table. I gave him a nice view of my derriere.

As I think I have mentioned, I know how to bait my hook. I know how to reel them in. I know when to wait.

"Won't you join me?" he volunteered. "I'm dining alone tonight."

Another two hours passed. He was thoroughly sauced by this time. I slipped a crushed Valium into his last drink. As we left I suggested we cab it home.

I brought my glass and his with me as we left.

I doubted he would do more than follow me, but I kept up my steady chatter.

"I guess I'll just get a room tonight . . . ."

He passed out in the cab but awoke and cooperated in a transfer to my car. I drove around. I removed his hair-piece and his tie and suit jacket.

I rolled up his sleeves and smudged a little dirt under his nails and on his shirt and exchanged his fancy moccasins for old sneakers from the flea market.

He no longer looked dignified or recognizable.

Then I propped him up and suggested we go upstairs. We were at my place. He was dazed and lethargic.

In my apartment, I handcuffed him to himself, ankle to wrist. Then I tied his knees so they were separated by a rope looped around his back. I crushed two more Valiums in honey and put them under his tongue.

Then I hoisted him on a blanket over the rim of my bathtub so his pulled-apart legs straddled the bathtub edge.

I brushed my teeth and washed at the sink. I put on my rubber gloves and lubricated them.

I abruptly shoved my gloved hand up his rectum.

He did try to speak. "Yes," he groaned.

"Like you did to little Carrie?" I cooed.

"Yes," he sighed.

I grabbed his penis in my hand, reaching under his ample belly.

"Which is better her ass or her front?" I asked.

"Equal," he laughed slightly and slurred this, so it sounded like "ekal."

He was erect immediately. I now had no doubt about his guilt.

I removed my hands and entered him.

I bashed against him mercilessly.

He protested and almost awoke.

"Later, again," he struggled a little, as he attempted to sound authoritative.

I pulled him out of the bathroom and placed him on the mattress, which I had pulled to the floor.

Again, I raped him. Each thrust harder. I withdrew and came in my own hand.

His rectum was much enlarged from previous affairs. Still he was bloodied.

I enjoyed my own justice with him.

I flipped him over and whispered in his ear, "After you get custody of her . . . . you'll really enjoy her, won't you?"

He didn't answer. I slapped him to at least a waking stupor.

"Custody could be fun, right?"

He smiled.

"Suck her little honey out, won't you?"

He laughed and mumbled, "Finger her too."

I crushed two more Valiums for under his tongue.

This time I released all his bonds.

I took a nail and heated it over the stove repeatedly. I burned into his thigh, "Fucks his kid."

Then I drew a penis and balls on his ass pointing to his anus.

I again bashed myself into him but this time I came with a shudder of complete delight.

I washed myself, ate a quart of ice cream and dressed him.

I gave him a strong drink, which he happily took and smeared some on his clothes.

Around dawn, we left my apartment, him in his new clothes and me in mine.

I delivered him to a Bowery corner. I drove back to the apartment. I straightened up. I was in excellent spirits.

His attaché case had nothing important in it. His wallet was filled with hundred dollar bills. I actually made a profit on the night.

I returned to my Helen a blond. I confiscated my new clothes and his by burning them in the basement and combining them with the root cellar earth.

I left the briefcase emptied in a dumpster in Manhattan the next day.

Several days later a headline read, "Society Judge Gives Up Custody Battle."

I guess he lived to appreciate my graffiti. I knew he wouldn't snitch to the authorities. He was too humiliated by his exposure.

Forgive my pun.

Chapter 33

FINALLY MY AVOIDANCE OF HELEN stopped. She put an end to it.

I came home to what I thought was an empty house. A note on the refigerator read:

Sara is at Helga's house for the day.
Love, Helen

I stripped naked and went to the basement. I blasted my music and worked out in front of my mirrors. I was in excellent humor and had been for over a month. The whole "custody victory" was great.

I liked what I saw in those mirrors. My backside was firm and well developed. I was lean and mean.

I posed myself with bright lights. I examined myself from every angle.

I was excited by my own strength and beauty. I became interested in arousing myself and put my body in exotic poses as if a slave to myself.

Imagine my shock when Helen called downstairs. She knew better than to just come uninvited into my space.

"Hungry?" she called out. "I'm home. I took a mental health day," she announced through the stairwell.

"Right up," I called back.

She was still in her nightgown.

The scar over her breast was lovely; on Helen's timid fragile body all violence, bruises, scars, were raised to high art. She was exquisite.

"Let's go to Cold Springs Harbor for the day," I announced.

She packed a picnic lunch for the car.

We visited the "Bear" shop and got Sara a huggy bear that giggled if you squeezed it.

Helen and I made a striking couple because of my size as compared to Helen's. We are both attractive.

Occasionally someone will think she is my daughter.

This is especially true since I have recently developed a shock of white hair at the temples. I leave that and a strand on top white, without blonde tint.

We spent a very satisfying afternoon browsing shops, eating cherry filled cordials, courting again.

Helen was wearing the little diamond ring I had given her a year or so back when we had reacquainted after the basement episode. She wore a huge straw hat with a pink chiffon band.

I called Helga and said I would pay her time and a half if she would keep Sara overnight. She agreed.

Helen and I arrived home relaxed. She broke out some white wine for us.

"Helen, I'm not drinking anymore," I told her. "I think I am an alcoholic."

I was surprised to hear myself say it out loud. I had not really even thought of it, up until that moment.

"Oh," she said and poured it down the sink.

I led her to the porch and we danced until the first stars were twinkling above.

I flipped the dim porch light on.

I held her close and slowly disrobed her.

She shuddered, not from the cold, but I draped the small yellow crocheted comforter over her shoulders anyway.

To see her covered above but nude below was amazing. I seated her on the swing, legs apart. I swung her while seated on my wicker rocker. I pushed her with my bare feet.

She looked up at the stars as if I was not there somehow. I don't like to be ignored—ever. I command attention in most situations by my height and good looks. As for Helen, she was mine as a royal subject was. I protected her as a king would but she must always be mindful of my superiority of station, my ownership and tolerance of her. I tilted her head down toward me. And I again pushed her.

She knew her mistake because she remained in this position. Then I noticed that she had tweezed her eyebrows. It gave her a whorish sophistication. I didn't like it.

"Did I give you permission to tweeze your eyebrows?" I asked her this sweetly and gently.

She didn't answer.

"Answer!" I bellowed.

I wasn't angry really. It was a matter of principle with me that she show respect.

"No," she whispered.

"Fine," I smiled. "Grow them back."

I can be very magnanimous.

Suddenly it escaped me, I didn't plan it.

"Whose picture do you carry in your wallet?"

She looked acutely anxious and puzzled. Then she relaxed.

"My brother," she finally responded.

"Brother?" I laughed heartily.

So she had a family. I waited for more information but it didn't come.

I carried her upstairs. No sedation was necessary. We were uncomplicated, sweet and finished in a twinkling.

I knew not to question her about her past. As I have said, her silence was a loud omission to me.

We held each other all night. There was a peacefulness and pure joy about that day which stands out in my mind.

A FEW DAYS later I visited my therapist to refill my prescriptions.

She asked me, "Are you feeling better than that last time?"

I was relaxed when I told her, "The old photo was Helen's brother."

"Did you ask her finally then?"

"Yes. It was silly of me to overreact," I said.

"Is he her older or younger brother?" she asked.

"I didn't ask." I said.

"Oh." She became quiet and pensive.

"I don't and never have asked Helen about her past; only her life with me matters . . . ." I volunteered. "Well, she's never talked about her family. I don't know where they live or if they're alive," I said.

"You're not curious?" she said.

"I respect her need for privacy on these matters . . . Frankly, I don't wish to know about them. They are not in her life or mine. I don't want my head cluttered with her memories. Her ghosts could become mine," I said after a prolonged silence.

"That's reasonable," she responded. "Why add ghosts?" she elaborated.

Adding ghosts was indeed a new perspective. I of course did have my own dark past to cope with.

"To have to push out Helen's ghosts would compete with who we are now together."

"You mean contaminate the present?" she said.

"Yes," I sighed.

This doctor was sharp. She kept her promise. We were in the here and now.

"How is your sobriety from alcohol going?"

"Fine," I lied. I had drunk heavily the night I had spent with the judge but I was back on the wagon.

"I had a slip," I finally admitted a few minutes later. "But I'm back on track."

"Making any A.A. meetings?"

I nodded. She gave me my usual prescriptions and we said goodbye until I needed her again.

Chapter 34

AFTER THE PHOTO INCIDENT, I lapsed into my usual routines. I noticed that the shingles were in need of repair after a harsh winter. It was an easy job— only five or six needed work, so I climbed up and just scaled the roof in a crawl.

Things were going well when several shingles which before seemed stable slid downward. I cascaded down and landed on my feet, then my back.

I lay prostrate, stunned. When I tried to get up, the pain was excruciating. I screamed out for Helen.

She was not home. We are a great distance from other houses. No one could hear me.

I managed to pull up on my knees. Although my back was in agony, I was unprepared for what happened next. When I attempted to stand, my ankles buckled under a combination of pain and the fact as I found out later, they were broken.

I lay there, a prisoner of pain and unable to move. I felt panic-stricken. Helen had gone into the town for a church bazaar and had brought Sara with her. It was an all-day affair which stretched to a potluck supper in the evening. I attempted to again crawl but the prolonged effort sent me into unbelievable pain. My heart was racing with fear and panic.

I tried to calm myself by lying still and breathing in and out deeply. It didn't work. I could feel my chest tightening as if a booted man was standing on it. It was that thought which made the situation worse.

Suddenly, I was no more there. I was in the attic. My father was standing over me one foot on my chest. I was naked. He had his hands clenched into a fist. There was blood on the fist—my blood. I was thrashing from side to side to release myself. He was laughing and kicking me. He was punching me in my side, yanking my penis. I was whimpering, now begging.

Then he was smiling beneficently, beaming with delight. He knelt down tenderly, his pants open.

"Take it," he commanded.

I choked until he was done. Then he was carrying me to the basement.

I awoke to the darkness and the bad smells. The same bad smells that came in memory, or were they real?

Terrible smells of sweat and him sticky and hot—smells that told me he had visited me. But I had no recollection. Mercifully I had passed out, so the only witnesses were the stains or marks. The pain lasted for days and so did most of all the smells, so that when I recovered, which inevitably I did, I spent hours scrubbing my little mattress with disinfectant to mask the odors.

But I couldn't mask them in my mind. They were demon stains, which could reoccur at unpredictable moments in school or sleep.

So that as I grew older— too big for him to abuse— I took to wearing aftershave and colognes and to buying perfumed spray.

I took a small sliver of perfumed soap to school. If I felt a panic attack coming on, I would sniff the fragrant soap. The panic was almost seizure-like, because it always was preceded by the smells—vivid, nauseating, and real to my core.

Sometimes, pain brought them on. Playing and falling hard once, one began.

A fight after school my nose bloody; the pain shifted. I discovered something new. In that instant of the fight, my defeat shifted to triumph; my rage took over—a power surged. I was beating "him"—the kid, and my father. I was winning. I was okay. I was in control, finally. The smells receded; the panic was gone. That day was a turning point in my existence.

Then I fell from the roof. On my back in pain, unable to move, a prisoner. I could not fight back. Again all control was stripped.

I shuddered and wept. Then I guess I passed out. Mercifully, my next memory is of my lovely Helen holding me in her arms, crying, begging me to wake up.

Chapter 35

I WAS TRANSPORTED TO THE hospital by ambulance. This was where Helen had given birth and was the "only show in town." After a month, I was released with casts on both ankles and a back brace for day and night use.

I could do very little for myself.

Helen would wash me. In the first few weeks home, we only washed the essentials. I was on painkillers as needed.

The problem was I felt like a caged animal. Helen could lift my head to feed me. I couldn't raise myself or sit up for another month.

I was reduced to babbling infancy. Although my captor was merciful, I was very depressed and underwent multiple panic attacks and fainting spells. So debilitating were these episodes that I finally called my doctor.

I explained without details that I had fallen and was restricted to my bed. I described my chest tightening and panic. She remembered the episode in her office.

"I can give you something, but it's similar to Valium. It will diminish or get rid of the panic, but it can be addictive if overused."

I liked the thought that it was similar to Valium. It would give me a little storehouse of prescription medication.

"I will use it cautiously," I answered.

"These two meds are used for alcohol withdrawal, but be careful, you don't want to substitute another addiction for alcohol do you?" she asked.

She must have thought I was an idiot.

"I'll be judicial in its use," I answered.

The word "judicial" reminded me of the repented judge I had used sedatives on. I was almost chuckling as I got off the phone.

Then I realized I had no way to get the prescription without Helen knowing.

I couldn't risk her knowing. So I just toughed it out. I called the pharmacy and asked them to hold the prescriptions until I was well enough to pick them up.

During the days after I was discharged, Helen took time off from work.

After three days, she had to return. I was left to Helga's occasional help or the use of a urinal by our bed. Helga would bring in food to me or fluff my pillow. But I detested taking her help.

She dwarfed me as I lay helpless. I hated her huge bosoms big bones, and unfriendly self. She went through the motions only.

I didn't want her help.

The illness didn't humble me. It festered me.

Poisonous fear crept into my every waking and sleeping moment.

In my dreams, I was tied in my bed in the basement. In my waking hours my dreams were reality, for I couldn't move.

Helen was cautious with me. She would give me choices about everything, even the mundane. "Do you want your tea on the left or right? What kind of cookie? How many?" she would ask.

I lay there and remembered things I had forgotten.

My teacher, Mrs. Denny, in fourth grade.

She noticed marks on my legs and bruises on my arms. I couldn't answer her questions, of course.

She would walk me partway home.

She was an odd bird with short, carrot-red hair styled like Julius Caesar. Her eyes were huge and she overly made them up. She penciled her lips with brown liner. Yeah, she was eccentric, you could say. But I liked that. She wore a guardian angel pin on her sleeve.

She would look up and flutter her long lashes and say, "Perfect love casteth out all fear." She meant God, I think.

But I remembered how her strange face would turn heavenward. Her eyes teared as if she knew what it meant in a deep, real way. "Companioning with Christ," she'd say. But I didn't understand her then.

As I lay in bed, unable to move, I think I finally heard her voice in a new way.

She meant she could see the fear I lived with. She was offering me her perfect love in God or from God. She was saying I needed faith to get me through the fear.

How could she understand how dark, how utterly without hope my basement was?

But my Helen was "perfect love which casteth out all fear . . . ."

In her some peace was possible.

One night I dozed in a twilight place. I saw Helen. She was wearing a blue lace corset. The cups were push-up, which bulged her breasts upward, the waist had stays and blue lacing that she had pulled tightly in. She had tiny blue lace panties under her lace garters and pale blue stockings also topped with lace. Strangely, she was wearing blue stiletto heels.

She crept by me so as not to wake me. I watched her fully—exposed, perfect backside as she bent to pick up the magazines on the floor and the dinner tray.

Where was she going in that outfit? This was my first thought.

Who was she dressing for?

I spoke hazily from my doze but my nerves were fully exposed, my adrenaline pumping.

Sweetly, I asked, "Helen, are you going out?"

She stammered, startled that I was awake. "I only thought to, well, you, if you want, well . . . ."

She didn't finish but let the sentence trail off.

She looked perplexed, almost comical.

I opened my arms to her. "Come to me, Helen," I said. She hesitated. She backed off, in fact. Something she would never have tried if I were not bedridden.

"I'll come back in later, a while . . .," she stammered off again, backing away.

I was not in pain. In fact, for several days, I had been able to hobble to the bathroom alone. I experimented alone, so I wouldn't humiliate myself if I failed in front of Helga or Helen.

I changed my tack with her.

"I'm feeling a terrible shooting pain down my back and leg . . . can you help me?"

She relaxed and put down the tray and magazines.

She leaned over me. Her breasts smelled wonderful. Her hair was squeaky clean, loose, and a little wild.

She stroked my head tenderly.

"Shall I readjust your pillow?" she asked, worried.

"Please . . ."

As she reached over me, I grabbed both her arms and pulled her close to me. You see, a man of two hundred and fifty pounds who is six feet five inches tall, even one who is debilitated, is no match for an eighty pound woman with one withered arm.

I yanked her so hard she screamed and lost her balance.

I yanked her on top of me.

With one hand I held her tightly. With the other I pulled away the flimsy pantie. I was in her almost instantly.

Rather than moving myself, I pulled her up and down, like a rag doll, until I spasmed into her.

I bit her breasts and her neck and yanked her hair until she cried. Then I stroked her head.

I loved her crying. I loved the red marks I made. I loved my power over her, even as I lay a patient in recovery.

I held her next to me until again my excitement and rage peaked.

I was surprised how I could repeatedly enjoy her in this new way. I felt such exquisite power over her, because I was so incapacitated, yet I could still master her. When I was finished, I held her tightly in silence. She sobbed intermittently.

Finally, when she fell asleep, I yanked her head back again when I knew she was undefended and half asleep and asked, "Why the sexy outfit? For who? Do you dare to cross me?"

She shook her head. Her lashes were moist. I saw Mrs. Denny for a split second.

"I did it for you, only you . . . because I missed you so . . . ."

Suddenly, I knew she spoke the truth.

I had been savage and cruel to the only one I've ever loved.

I think I stared into her eyes in complete silence and shock.

The balance of power shifted momentarily. I was just a small, petty, mean man. I was embarrassed to have hurt her. I kissed her slack, open mouth.

"Oh Helen, I'm so sorry," I whispered. "What have I done?"

A moment passed and she replied, "Only what you needed to do . . . ."

Chapter 36

WHEN THE NEXT DOCTOR'S APPOINTMENT was over, he had removed the cast and declared me cured.

"You will need physical therapy for several weeks. But the worst is over. Gradually, build up the use of your legs and stay away from strenuous lifting for at least a year."

This was a small price to pay to have back my life.

I was able to return to work and a fully normal routine.

I went for physical therapy three times a week.

I refrained from household repairs and was cautious not to lift even Sara. Instead, I coaxed her into my lap.

I remembered to pick up my extra arsenal of sedatives from the pharmacy.

I was back on track.

The bite marks on Helen faded quickly, all except one on the same breast that had been burned. As I have said, such marks were raised to high art on Helen. On her milky white, perfect body, they were punctuation, a contrast which heightened the effect of her obvious femininity and vulnerability. I loved this. But the bite mark bothered me, because it reminded me of my own flawed temperament. I had wronged her that night. Like the old photo, I had read too much into nothing. This, combined with having twisted her ankle, distressed me. I was losing some metaphysical battle with my own evil.

Chapter 37

RELIEF ABOUT THE OLD PHOTO combined with a desire to make amends to Helen. I planned a Caribbean cruise to please her.

I had never seen Helen in a swimsuit. Sara had never frolicked at a beach.

I would imagine Helen on a chestnut horse, her red hair blowing behind her. I could lick droplets of salty perspiration from her back and between her breasts.

This would be a time to spin dreams, to taste deeply of her most wonderful healing tenderness.

I needed her alone with me but I would cherish Sara with us. Helen would no doubt create another album of our little time together.

The place I finally reserved was a five-day cruise with nightclub dancing, pool and child care activities.

Once we arrived on the island, Sara would have horseback riding, crafts, swimming, day and evening childcare. Still, I suggested that Helga come. This way the nights would be our own. We would have time with Sara and alone.

The rooms were tiny but a small space with Helen was fine.

We didn't gamble. Seeing Helen in her swimsuit was my main activity. I bought it for her. It was a crocheted deep blue. Frankly, it barely covered her. Her tiny bottom just barely skimmed out. Her breasts needed no support. It was merely to camouflage the obvious.

Her red toenails and fingernails were fabulous. She clung to my arm, a little shy about the suit I had selected. She draped a large scarf at her waist like a sarong. When she was outside of the pool, I pulled it off sometimes.

She would lounge on the deck chair beside me holding my hand. I wore dark glasses so I could watch others study my Helen. One man actually was aroused visibly and had to sit down.

Sara splashed in the shallow end of the pool. I gave her rides across on my back. She splashed water at me as I floated on my back, while I pretended to sleep.

I hadn't taken Helen dancing since that first time in which I had beaten up the guy in the club. This time would be different, I reasoned.

We had been together nearly six years. I should be more confident about leaving her for a few minutes.

I selected her wardrobe for our cruise. One dress, a gold lamé fabric cut on the bias, was strapless, a slit up the side stopped just above her knee. I got her spaghetti strap sandals also in gold with a thin heel. She needed no bra with this outfit.

At my insistence, she wore no underwear. You could see her perfect backside and nipples, but it was not transparent. With her red nails and hair, my God, she was a goddess. I got her dangling diamond earrings. She was dressed like a movie star at a Hollywood debut.

When we entered the dining room for dinner, there was an audible hush as heads turned to gaze at my Helen.

I wore a white tuxedo with a yellow cummerbund, to complement her outfit.

We were treated like royalty by the cruise staff.

Some women after a meal would bulge in such a dress. Not my Helen. She ate like a bird. A few shrimp, a slice or two of pineapple, and she was done.

I whirled her on the dance floor, dipping her back, making her breathless with excitement. All I could think about was her nudity under the provocative gown. When I dipped her I watched the men try to peek under her dress, the slit drawn upward. This excited me. She was mine. To have this prize that all coveted pleased me.

I was damp with anticipation of our later games.

I didn't leave her alone for a minute. When I went to the men's room, I suggested she go to "powder her nose" in the ladies' room. If she went, I waited outside for her. There need be no unpleasantness. I was watchful and more cautious. Experience had taught me to hover protectively around my Helen on these public occasions.

We closed the dance floor the first night.

It was almost three in the morning. We didn't have to worry about curfews or waking for Sara. Helga was there to help.

Chapter 38

THE THIRD NIGHT, ON BOARD they staged an adaptation of the ballet *Swan Lake,* by Tchaikovsky.

A beautiful princess is trapped by an evil enchanter. He casts a spell. She becomes a white swan, but for a few hours each night by the light of the moon, she is set free to dance as a human.

She is discovered dancing by the handsome Prince Zigfried. Her little tutu trembles; her arms and head are transformed before our eyes. She flaps her arms as delicate wings. Zigfried and she dance a dance of fearful delight as she becomes more human. He dips her, catching her by her tiny waist just as she swoons.

Her legs acrobatically spread. She balances on one tiny toe shoe, the other perilously pointed above them. He grabs her raised leg and rests it on his broad shoulders.

Then he spins her on her one toe shoe, barely holding her waist, her raised leg now pointed alone and free.

Then, as if falling from a great height, she tilts into his arms—caught. Her delicate legs scissor together again. She falls trustingly into his outstretched arms as he waits below on the dance floor, catching her two legs in time. He raises her above him, then dips her head downward, her crossed legs now above. He is twirling her again until she lands on one toe, the other pointed behind.

Suddenly, he clasps her face to face. She raises both legs to lock them around his waist as he tilts her to the right to kiss her.

Released, she again trembles. The sun is rising. Nearly dawn, now, the evil enchanter appears, his mask and black cape lined in red satin. He raises his cape high, a powerful demon ready to firmly capture her to him.

She quivers, again, becoming a swan. Her head inclines and rests on her shoulder. Her arms raise as wings over her head to flap noiselessly without flight.

She twirls into the red cape of the enchanter, who closes his cape around her.

Helen watched noiselessly too. It was breathtaking. For the first time, I understood myself.

Helen is the beautiful trapped swan. I am the handsome Zigfried; in love with her, wishing to possess her.

I am, also, the evil enchanter. I have trapped my lovely swan, so no other may possess her. I have powers to hold her, control her, and draw her to me.

She is beautiful as she moves between her two selves, the trapped bird and princess.

I am both her prince who wishes to release her and her evil enchanter who wishes to keep her captive.

This new insight into my passion for Helen became a new obsession. If I could have swallowed her whole, I would have. She could cure me if I could swallow her whole as a magic potion. I couldn't get deeply enough inside her.

I wanted to bury myself so deep inside her as to be reborn of her. I understood the evil enchanter too well. He had an illness, an incompleteness. To live, he needed his swan.

I too was not wicked. I was possessed of an illness, an incompleteness.

I could not stop myself. Day and night I hammered into Helen. I couldn't get deep enough. No position brought us into sufficient contact.

I could not stop kissing her, touching her, absorbing her.

She thrilled me and eluded me.

ON THE FOURTH night the chef approached me. "Could I do a portrait of her in ice? For the festival night the last evening of the cruise?" he added.

"Would she need to pose?" I asked.

"Oh, no sir, who could forget her? I will do it from memory with your permission, respectfully . . . A Goddess rising from the sea . . . ."

He surprised us by depicting her in exactly this way.

Helen protested, "Surely, that's not me?"

He had captured her beauty, fragility, the Goddess I worshipped.

I photographed his work.

Then I asked him, "Can you complete such a breath-taking sculpture more permanently?"

"How, sir?" he asked.

"In stone," I suggested.

"Soap stone," he said.

"Same as you have done tonight," I suggested.

"Remember, sir, it is the impermanence of the ice that imparts the magic. If I could do her in precious crystal, now that would do justice to her . . . ."

I could see his point.

I tipped him handsomely but was pleased to have the colored photo of her, instead.

She posed in the gold lamé dress next to the ice sculpture he had created. I had it blown up and framed.

The Caribbean was as I imagined, but more beautiful, because my two treasures were with me.

The day I saw in my mind's eye was pale and lifeless compared to seeing Helen on a horse. I lifted her onto her chestnut red horse. The owner of the stable explained that the horses were so docile, small children could ride them. They would follow the trail no faster than a trot, always returning to the stables when done.

Helen wore my white tailored shirt over black jeans. A strand of pearls adorned her throat. I unbuttoned one button more than she would have. In her ears were pearl and diamond studs. She sparkled more than any glimmer in the sun.

As she galloped, she threw her head back, laughing out loud with such abandon, she seemed truly free. She tossed her helmet down and ran her winged arm through her full red hair. As is the case with all red hair its chemistry would seem to alter depending on the season. It was more fair, seeming to be streaked with light.

I rode alongside her, wishing I could ride backwards to see her more completely. Toward the end of the trail, I held her reins in my hand. We slowed to a mutual walk and I leaned in to kiss her.

On impulse I lifted her onto my horse to sit sidesaddle, embracing her.

That evening we danced until midnight, but retired early. As we walked back along the beach, the stars seemed mine to hold. In a nook of shaded rock and trees, I held her to me.

She wore a red chiffon dress. The wide shear skirt I had selected for its fullness on the dance floor. The delicate slip top clung lightly, thin stain ribbon straps at each shoulder crossed in the back. Her tiny matching underwear I, of course, selected as well.

It was easy to steal her secretly by lifting the billowy fabric. I thought I must surely have gone to heaven. No alcohol or drugs could be so potent. To complete a perfect seduction, I carried her back.

The next day, we brought Sara out on the horse. She sat with me, and I straddled her tiny body. I extended control over my natural bodily reactions from her movement against me as the horse galloped. I was concentrating on the smell of her hair and body, the aroma only a baby or small child can have. In my periphery I could see my Helen.

Could a man be happier than I was?

Chapter 39

IT WAS RAINING ON OUR last day of vacation. We went to the beach anyway. The horizon was clear. The sun was shining yet the rain came like tears on a happy occasion.

Sara was digging up the sand and pushing it up into a castle. Helen was helping, molding buckets of wet sand into shapes. The rain washed it away as quickly as they worked. They didn't care; just the joy of doing it together was enough.

I watched from my chair. We were alone on the beach.

Helen's wet clothes were sticking to her. Sara looked like an antique doll, too much played with.

As they dug deeper, water filled the hole and caved it in.

Sara lifted a bone from the sand.

Helen looked at it and held it up to me. I studied it.

It looked almost human, but I think it was a lamb shank.

Then it happened. I was unconscious. Helen shaking me and Sara crying.

When I looked up into their faces, I saw it again. The old tree in the orchard, the hollow stump. The smell rotten flesh.

I rolled to my side and vomited.

Helen got me to my knees and then my feet.

She sat me back in the chair and fell to her knees before me. She held me and rocked me.

"Mommy knows what to do," she repeated, and kissed my eyes. The rain was stopping. Sara climbed on my lap. So that was it, then. I would have to return one more time to the old farm.

Chapter 40

WE DECIDED TO TAKE THE jet home. We were exhausted. Helga needed to get back to her house.

We had knocked ourselves out pleasuring and relaxing. Frankly, it was good to get home.

Sara's sleep schedule was disrupted for about a week; so was mine.

Then things settled back.

Work continued to be easy, except for the weekly meetings. Fortunately, I could bring Mrs. Percy to those. At first my boss balked, but I insisted. She would make notes on particular areas of follow-up that might not appear in the general minutes. This actually worked in my favor, as he thought I was highly motivated and professional in demeanor. He even said so.

The second day back I decided to stay late to "supervise" the evening staff. I wanted a few hours to look for the vagabond, in fact.

As I sat in my office saying goodnight to the last of the day staff, I heard pitiful meowing.

I thought I was hallucinating. We were, after all, on the third floor.

Finally, I got curious, so I went downstairs. Ours was the only light on and window open.

"Kitty, oh kitty," I squeaked.

Immediately a calico boy kitty appeared. It ran to me meowing and rubbing. I bent to stroke it and it jumped on my lap. It buried its little head in my armpit and began kneading me with its front paws. I continued to stroke it. To my surprise, it climbed up my suit jacket and wrapped itself around my neck. So loving was this unusual cat that when I put it down, it jumped back on my lap.

I carried it under my jacket to the deli and bought a can of tuna.

I put the open can down in the alley. Then I scooted out of there quickly while it was distracted, eating.

I decided to go home after all.

Most of the evening I thought about its green eyes and golden orange and charcoal markings. Its face was flat—looking and its coat shiny. Maybe it had been abandoned.

The next day I was curious. When evening came I went out to the back. I saw no cat, so I again made a squeaky voice calling "kitty."

It darted out, quickly meowing as if I was an old friend. It had been hiding in a hole in the base of the building. Its fur was covered in tiny shards of broken glass and sand. Again it jumped up on my lap to begin its love ritual.

It reminded me of my lovely hen of boyhood. It was the same color. Maybe I'm a sucker for the extraordinary. I brought it upstairs with a can of tuna and closed my office door.

Then I called Helen with my crazy story.

"Bring it home; we can take it to the vet tomorrow. We can see how Puffy likes it," she replied.

Helen was, as usual, very agreeable to my leanings. When I got it home Helen gave it a flea bath using Puffy's stuff and wrapped it in a towel. When she brought it out, it was pretty scared. It was shaking and urinated on Helen's lap.

Puffy came over to sniff, curious about this little spectacle. Then she started licking him. The kitten noticeably relaxed, so Helen put him down. He looked like a drowned rat. Puffy flopped down next to it while he groomed himself.

The experiment was working. The next day Helen took it to the vet for shots. "Kitty Business" was now a family member.

Chapter 41

I HAD AVOIDED THE OBVIOUS. More than two weeks went by before I took my leave of Helen to return to the old farm. I was almost afraid to drive out. Suppose I passed out behind the steering wheel? I ate a good breakfast and chose less—traveled roads. I also took half a Valium.

I had forgotten how grim the farm was in daylight. Without the farmhouse it was worse. The burned building had not been cleared. Rain and wind had knocked it down further. A storm had knocked a dead tree over it, shrouding it in more havoc and death.

Behind me stood the old barn and farther still the orchard.

My knees were trembling. For the first time I took the Mellaril. I opened the capsule and poured part onto my tongue. I swilled the bitter powder with soda. I had brought a metal shovel and bucket. Looking down at them reminded me of that day at the beach.

During the walk I felt I understood, the death row walk. My legs held back as if shackled. I moved forward but wanted to turn back to run.

I heard the sound of my own fear as the beating of my heart flooded my ears.

There it was, the hollow stump. Once a tall tree, it stood an immovable memorial to a previous time.

I HAD BEEN in the orchard with my dog Lucky. Lucky was a rescue dog, tiny wire-haired, almost a Chihuahua. I had smuggled it down to my room and out to the orchard for over a month.

The tree hollow was big, just the right size for a tiny dog. He had huge ears but one was torn from where he had gotten stuck under the barbed-wire fence at the back of the farm.

The orchard was not income producing for my father. It was a leftover of nature. Since it was fall, the apples had begun ripening and falling to the ground. Lucky had a natural dog house in the tree hollow. It was about eighteen inches wide. I had put an old towel inside. His bowl of food and water were close outside. I was holding him on my lap. While I stroked him with one hand, my other hand picked up ripe apples to eat. I took only one bite out of each apple, then tossed it aside. As the sun filtered through the leaves, I lay back, my belly full. Lucky crawled up to my chest and licked my face. I took a bite from one last apple. I gazed up into the tree leaves to the specks of blue sky and remaining apples.

My father leaned over me and grabbed my Lucky, tossing his tiny body against the huge tree with such force that his neck snapped.

Even as I rose to save him, it was over.

"Wasting apples, you pig?" He slapped me.

I think I was five years old.

I couldn't feel the slaps. I couldn't see him. I could only see my Lucky lifeless, his blood on the hideous tree.

I ran to Lucky and held him in my arms, covering him with kisses, hoping to make it all better again.

Within a second or two, my father had retrieved his electric saw from the pick-up truck. He began cutting my tree down, cutting through the very hollow of Lucky's doghouse.

Then he grabbed Lucky from me and stuffed him like garbage into the hollow from the top. He ripped handfuls of grass out with sod attached and threw them on top, then pushed his booted foot down hard to pack the dirt.

How did I get home or did I get home that night?

My eyes had photographed it all but could it be the product of an overactive imagination? What of the rotted flesh? What drove me to know the truth?

I stood there seeing it all as it had been. The fallen tree, old blood still staining it. The little towel jutting from the side of the hollow stump.

I took the shovel and began digging out the top. Anger took over. I didn't faint. My face was hot. There was Lucky, his bones and tiny collar.

Stunned, I stood staring into the past.

I gently recovered his shallow grave. The small gold cross I had around my neck was Sara's. I grasped it, not for reassurance, but to pull it off.

I dropped the tiny gold cross into his resting place and wept.

Chapter 42

I DROVE HOME THAT NIGHT numb.

As I walked through the door, Helen gasped and ran to me.

She covered my face with kisses.

I sunk into the recliner.

She removed my shoes and socks, then my remaining clothing. Then she drew a hot bath.

She disrobed. All in silence. A powerful earnestness was in all that she did.

I was led as an initiate to a sacred rite. No baptism could do what Helen attempted.

Fully immersed in the hot water, the aroma of strawberry oil around me, she scrubbed me. She began using a pair of rough sponges. Suds and oil, she rubbed as if to unseal all that I was or had been. There was brutality to this honest love. She was making war with my ghosts, the very ones she saw that made her gasp. My face, ears, and scalp, then my neck and shoulders down to my toes. She rinsed me and repeated it. This time she used her hands.

She guided me to our bed. Naked still, she kissed my feet and toes. As if worshipping me, she placed her one hand on my head and purposefully moved over me with her wing from head to toe. Occasionally, she shook off some invisible slough of energy.

Next, she oiled my body with yet another aroma, lubricating my most delicate areas. She kissed me fully as if to ingest me and make me into her own cells.

I could not tell where I left off and she began. We were one. Yet so passive was I that I believed I was again that frightened five year old, not really comprehending the love, the all consuming fire which sought to burn the evil I had endured.

Not a word passed between us.

This was beyond arousal. She had performed an exorcism.

She repeated it all again on the back of my body.

No nook, no private place was left to feel dirty, violated, or harmed.

Only goodness, cleanness, holiness remained.

I, the small child, looked in wonder at this naked angel.

As she worked, she cried. Her eyes filled with tears which spilled onto my naked body. They mixed with my own.

She too had been violated, torn. She too fought back my ghosts but as an adult, mother, wife and lover who would have no one assault her loved ones.

Her power to defend me, to protect what she loved, I had only glimpsed.

She was a priestess and warrior as only mother love can be.

Finally, exhausted, she fell on top of me. We embraced as equal adults.

No arousal, no pleasure I had ever sought or known compared with the purity of this love.

The next day we did not discuss it. No words were necessary. Indeed, they would trivialize what had taken place.

PERHAPS STRESS FROM my new promotion or the in flooding of memories precipitated my illness.

A few nights later, I awoke with agonizing pain. I didn't wake Helen. I took a hot bath and half a Valium. The pain subsided to a dull throbbing.

My groin and one testicle hurt. I had excruciating pain in my back as well. I psychologized. Recent events had reminded me of times in which these areas had been assaulted.

I went to work a little fuzzy from the sedative. By noon, I was in agony. So much pain did I endure that I broke out in a sweat. I could think of nothing else.

Finally, I called Helen, wise Helen.

"Kidney stones," she pronounced. "I'm coming right over to get you." She hung up.

I called Mrs. Percy into my office.

"You look quite ill," she said.

"Tell me about it," I replied.

"Can I call a doctor?" she asked.

"I think I need a urologist," I said.

Helen came within ten minutes. The cab she arrived in waited downstairs. She helped me down to it. She already had called ahead to a midtown urology practice.

When we arrived, they took me immediately. Helen had explained everything by phone in advance.

My temperature was 104 degrees. I was perspiring and shaking in chills.

"You can go to the emergency room or we can do the procedure here," the doctor said.

"We're here," she answered for me. "Do it now." She was definitive.

"He has a urinal blockage. The urine can't escape, so it's backing toxins into his system."

"Just do it," she said again.

"We will sedate him with a Valium drip and dilate him so he can pass the stone," the doctor said.

Helen signed a release.

I was up on a table draped butt naked, my own legs in stirrups. The doctor was Chinese and very gentle. He was able to calm me. "You will pass out the moment I begin the drip. You will feel nothing and awaken better . . . Afterward, you take me for Chinese food . . . Yes?"

He made me smile despite the misery of the situation.

I looked to Helen.

"She may stay," he said.

Helen held my hand.

Mercifully, it was just as he described.

When I awoke, Helen was next to me and he was helping me lower my legs. After a brief sit in the procedure room, he helped me into a waiting area.

"You must wait here until all sedation is out of your system. I have prescribed an antibiotic and a painkiller. Naturally, if a reoccurrence of urinal pain occurs, return or call immediately. I can be reached twenty-four hours a day," he ended.

I felt tearfully grateful. Again, someone, an utter stranger, had offered me a kindness I had never known within my own family.

"Expect a great discomfort as you pass your first urine, within the first hour or so. There will be a lot of blood. This is natural, as we have dilated your urethra," he reassured me.

"They say what you have is the closest to childbirth any man can experience," he chuckled.

A few days later, I dropped by with a gift certificate for a Chinese restaurant in the neighborhood for my good doctor.

Chapter 43

THE NEXT FEW DAYS, I had recurring pain, but thankfully not of the previous magnitude.

I woke for several nights in pain, scared but not wishing to disturb Helen.

I'd get into a hot tub and sip hot tea. Sometimes the painkillers didn't help. I took to drinking huge amounts of water. The doctor said this would dilute my urine and help pass the gravelly stones. Helen on several nights woke to make my tea or draw my bath.

On one occasion I was in pain, but my love of my angel was so great I became aroused.

Imagine me in pain from kidney stones, yet so smitten I could still make love to my Helen.

We laughed about it for weeks later.

As I lay in my bed moaning, Kitty Business would get up on the bed and start kneading me with his paws. He sat on my stomach, too. Oddly enough, this calmed me despite the pain.

I missed quite a bit of work, but after two weeks, I seemed to have passed the stones.

Helen got a book on kidney stones. She instructed Helga and me on which foods to avoid.

I had to pee into a little cup for a month and filter it. This was done in the hopes of catching a stone.

A month later, the doctor pronounced what Helen had surmised. The stones were a mix of several kinds.

Helen began cooking most of my meals and sending lunch. She also prepared a huge bottle of much diluted cranberry juice. I drank a glass every hour.

The cat had endeared itself to me by its attentiveness to me during my illness, so when it began crawling into our bed at night, I let it be. It sat on my legs at first, then during the night it would shift to my pillow next to my head. Sometimes its purring woke me.

Chapter 44

My boss called me into his office after several months in my new job. I figured my frequent absences had gotten me fired.

He looked stilted and embarrassed.

"We have a new client who has written a book which we believe will be a best seller. The main character is a small white mouse. I would like you to do the final editing on his book."

"My problem is this . . . ." He reached down under his desk to produce a tiny plastic cage. In it was an albino mouse with red eyes.

"He has to have surgery and requests that we care for his treasured mouse."

"But surely sir, he would be . . . safer boarding with a veterinarian," I responded.

"True, but he is unreasonable, he requests that I, that is, 'we,' care for his mouse. Since I believe you mentioned you have a country house and several pets, I thought . . .," he drifted.

"Why not?" I answered. "I have a cat and dog, why not a mouse for a few days?" I figured Helga could take care of it. I was relieved not to be fired. He then produced a shopping bag filled with mouse necessities.

It turned out Helga was frightened of mice. Helen had difficulty manipulating the mouse and cage, so it fell to me.

I had to change its box every few days.

At night it ran continuously on a little treadmill. It stored its food in an empty toilet paper roll in the cage. If I came down during the night and opened the refrigerator, the mouse emitted a high pitched squeak. I would drop a kernel of corn into its cage as a reward for its genius.

When I stuck my hand into his cage the first time to clean out his box, trying to transfer him to a little cardboard box, he bit me, drawing blood. I couldn't even fling the little critter off of me. He held on like a pitbull.

Finally, I got him off by dropping my hand back into the cage. He shrieked the whole time as if I was the wicked one. He was a real character.

If it hadn't been for our important client, I would have set it loose in the woods.

Finally, a week later, my boss took him back with a thanks and handed me the manuscript I was to edit, called "Mouse and Me: An Autobiography."

Apparently, "mousey," or "Percival," was similar in behavior to his owner. Somehow, this guy had been able to weave his life story around his adventures with the mouse.

I didn't think much of the manuscript, but it wasn't my judgment call. Believe it or not, it did become a best-seller.

Chapter 45

MY YOUNG HOMELESS FRIEND WHOM I had rescued turned up a few months later. He was more together than I remembered him. For one thing he wasn't psychotic. He was actively drinking again, however. He didn't remember me. I passed him on more than one occasion but he didn't show any recognition.

I followed him for a few days. He was staying at a cheap hotel near the East River in lower Manhattan. It was little more than a flophouse. He was still picking up men. He had gained a little weight but otherwise was still in bad shape.

I zeroed in on him by asking him if he had the time.

He smiled alluringly.

"For what?" he asked.

"For us," I responded.

"Your place?" he asked.

This time he wasn't rubbing up against door frames, at least.

"We can get a room . . ., " I offered.

"Fine." He fell into step with me.

"How about dinner first?" I asked.

"You're paying, mister," he smiled. His beautiful smile was marred by a tooth which, previously there, was now missing.

I took him to a steak house on Eighty-sixth Street with a cheap fixed price. He got a huge meal, including potatoes and garlic bread.

I watched him eat in silence. Occasionally, he looked up, smiled, and went back to eating.

He was more subdued and less sexually preoccupied. No longer the rabid dog in heat, he was more of a businessman.

"What about a movie first?" I asked.

"You gotta pay extra for that time," he said without hesitation. I could smell the alcohol on his breath.

"I'll pay for your sobriety," I volunteered. I surprised myself.

"You gotta be kidding," he laughed out loud.

"You afraid I'll miss something in your little tricks?" he asked.

"Maybe," I said.

"Hell, I ain't been sober for months," he said.

"Do you remember ever being sober?" I asked.

"Well, vaguely," he muttered. "It's overrated, mister. What's your angle, anyway?" He was cautious now.

"I want you sober when I have you and I'll pay handsomely for it," I said.

"It takes time to get sober," he said defensively.

"I've got time," I answered.

"That time's gonna cost me in earnings," he stated.

"I'll pay you a hundred a day for nothing if you go through detox. It's your call."

"How much do you want me sober?" he asked.

"How much do you want to be sober?" I countered.

"Right now, not much," he answered.

"I won't turn you back out on the street," I answered.

"Oh, I'll be just for your pleasure?" he asked.

"Not quite."

"You run a legitimate front?" he asked, almost smug again.

"No. I'll send you upstate with the monks if you get your sobriety. Then it's up to you," I answered.

"I ain't promising anything," he hissed.

"One day at a time," I said.

"Don't fuck with my head, just my body." He was again angry. He started walking away.

No one walks away from me. I'm in control.

"Five hundred?" I said quietly.

"No sobriety?" he turned only his head.

"I just want my money's worth." I changed my tone.

"That's more like it, mister." He was back on familiar turf.

"The Washington Hotel, you come up to Room 28." I had already reserved one. "Let's go. Walk in front of me." He liked my command of him.

He walked with a slight limp. I hadn't remembered.

One foot appeared swollen, his jeans skimmed above his ankle. He swaggered, but he was compliant.

Once in the hotel, I asked what he wanted to drink.

"Whiskey," he spat out.

He looked ridiculous and tiny. His tough posturing made it funnier.

As I've said, I'm over 250 pounds and 6 feet, 5 inches. He was only about five feet, a youngster not even finished growing.

"Take a shower. Use this." I gave him de-lousing shampoo.

"Look, I'm clean," he protested.

"My money, my call," I reminded him.

When his whiskey came, I laced it with half a Valium. He drank it nude. I stayed dressed.

"I want another one," he demanded.

"Soon." I crossed my arms over my chest.

"Lie down with these pillows under your behind," I instructed him.

Now his glossy eyes took on that knowing look I remembered and despised.

"Play with yourself," I said.

He loved this. His eyes fluttered, closed.

"Look at me," I told him.

His eyes could not stay open. His effort at arousal started, then failed him.

Now he was mine, on my terms.

I slapped another Valium under his tongue. Then I went to work. I had taken the room for five days. When I returned, he still slept.

I disrobed and got into bed with him. I inspected his body. It was less damaged than before, although some wounds never heal.

One foot was swollen and blistered from badly-fitting shoes and long standing. The tooth was freshly broken off, probably in a fight. His behind was still torn.

I went through his pockets and was surprised to discover a vial of Tegretol and a clinic appointment card.

Suddenly I was frightened. I got dressed and went outside to a pay phone. I called Bellevue Pediatric Emergency Room.

"Triage nurse, please."

I can be commanding.

"My teenage son's on Tegretol. He's been drinking and taken two Valiums. Is there any danger?"

"Definitely, sir. Let me put you on to our doctor on call."

Moments later, a foreign doctor spoke.

"Your son has overdosed?"

"Not suicidal, stupidly . . .," I said.

"You better bring him in."

"Can't," I said. "He's passed out."

"Slap him awake if possible. You can always call an ambulance."

"He's an alcoholic, but he's getting Tegretol from your out-patient clinic . . . ."

"Stop the Tegretol," he said. "He could stop breathing or convulse," the doctor continued.

"Would he be hospitalized or just observed?" I asked.

"We would immediately admit him," the doctor said.

"Look," I lied, "he's just an acquaintance, but he's in big trouble. Can you still admit him?" I asked.

"Definitely," he said. "How will I know him?" the doctor asked.

"The I.D. in his wallet says 'John Doe' and he has the Tegretol bottle," I hung up.

My little friend was snoring; no signs of distress were visible.

I fondled him and released myself. Then I dressed him.

I slapped him. He was able to stand, but his speech was unintelligible. I walked him downstairs. It was about three in the morning. I hailed a cab to Bellevue Hospital.

I brought him into the Pediatric Emergency Room and left. The name on his medication was "Bill Smith." I doubted this was his real name. I had stuffed a note describing him as John Doe and his recent "medications."

There was nothing to link us if he didn't make it. I hoped he would.

Chapter 46

HELEN WAS PROMOTED TO "NORTHEAST Regional Director of Children's Publications." Hot title, right? The snag was she had to travel, sometimes overnight. Could I tell her not to accept a promotion which brought her into the big bucks? Damn straight, I wanted to. But I decided to watch and wait.

If Helen was going to be away from the house occasionally for a day or two, I could probably handle it. Especially if I had a little extra "no explanations" play time. Problem was, I could not risk increased time with Sara. If Helen was gone overnight and days at a time, I could not step into Sara's life more.

"Helen, I'm not against your success. In fact, you deserve it, but it is not seemly or prudent to give Sara over to my care more frequently," I said.

"But you're home in the daytime, most of the time," she answered. "We can switch Helga's days to be when you're working overtime, and add an evening occasionally," she replied.

This is what I meant about Helen detaching from Sara sometimes. Her grip of reality seemed a little tenuous at times.

"Helga will have to be here five days and the evenings you need to travel," I said.

"But it's so expensive . . .," she pleaded.

Sara was due to enter nursery school full-time, 8:30 - 2:00 p.m., in September, but what if she was sick? What if I had a need to watch her more? What if she was feverish and needed my doctoring? Get my drift?

Sara was verbal now. In theory, she could describe to others my little ways. She could remember now: to tell, to replay in her child's mind, to grow in the knowledge of a twisted tree.

She could end up the legacy my father had left behind.

Lord knows she was lusciously beautiful. Her strawberry-blonde hair to her shoulders, perfectly formed, her dark eyes and lashes seductive in the way child porn stars are alone capable.

I took Sara out of her bed. She was sleeping. My attentions didn't wake her. I had given her Benadryl before bed.

I brought her into the living room, then decided on the porch swing.

I laid her down. Helen watched in horror. I tied her wrist to the right side and her leg to the left. I spread her legs apart but didn't remove her underwear.

"Well, Helen. Helga or me?" I repeated.

This was the furthest I'd gone with Helen by way of almost confessing my worst proclivities and fears.

I didn't wait for her answer. I quickly removed the little restraints and carried her back to bed.

When I returned, Helen was standing on the porch, still. She was wringing her hands, pale, saliva on her chin, her eyes glazed.

"Speak!" I screamed.

She couldn't. She was gone. Far gone to a land I had almost glimpsed on the night she threw the spaghetti.

I changed my approach. I came closer. I stroked her face. She trembled, but she was not responding to me.

An inner drama now unreeled, a clip from a distant documentary.

She was watching it. Her eyes darted left to right, up then down. Her hands clenched into fists.

Then she began to punch me in the face. I stepped back, rather than restraining her or reciprocating. I was evolving, don't you think?

When I stepped back, she moved forward, fighting ghosts— not me.

Then it was over.

She collapsed on the floor. She had wet herself, again. So she had little episodes, too. Not dissimilar to my own.

What smells, tastes, what unarticulated pictures replayed in her mind at such times?

I was horrified. I wanted no ghosts in our life together. My own were enough, and her focus must be on me only. I could not tolerate our relationship being contaminated. I could not, I would not compete with any man or event, past or present.

I had gone too far.

It was my fault.

Obviously, I had won my point.

Helga would be offered a handsome raise for occasional evenings, as needed.

A few days later, I approached my employer. I would accept his offer. I would be willing to try the promotion, if he still needed me.

I reasoned that I needed to stay busy. I wanted to increase the challenge for myself. After all, I wasn't drinking, right? It would be an experiment only.

That night of Helen's flashback ordeal, I cleaned her up. I lay her on the bed. She was gone without a sedative. I slipped a Valium under her tongue. When I touched her, she stiffened like she had when I had last tried my little basement games.

All right, then. She had suffered enough. My goal was not to make her suffer. She was my light at the end of an eternal tunnel, my angel.

After about an hour, I returned. She was surely more relaxed now. I stroked her cheek. She stiffened again. I took her in my arms like an infant and rocked her. I sang her the lullaby Sara's little mobile played.

I carried her in my arms naked back and forth. She remained stiff.

I lay her down again. I slipped a Mellaril under her tongue with some honey. I put on soft music and waited.

She twitched, she stiffened, she clenched her fists. Finally, another hour passed; she relaxed.

Chapter 47

SO OUR LITTLE FAMILY BEGAN a new chapter.

As much as I detested Helga, I also was grateful for her help. I decided to tell her.

Helga let herself in that morning. I was waiting, framing my words.

She seemed surprised that I was home.

I waited until she had changed. She had a habit of changing to a nurse's outfit and white lace shoes before beginning her day. I suppose it reflected some kind of pride in her professional role.

I watched her. She watched me. I sipped my coffee. She had baked a crumb cake. It was still hot. She cut me a slice without asking and sat down. She knew something was up.

"Helga, I . . . We would like to express our appreciation for all your help," I began.

She shrugged dismissively.

I continued. "Were it not for you, I— we, would be distressed for Sara . . . ." I stopped.

She was staring at me.

"Well, we would appreciate your help for an occasional evening. Helen will try a new promotion out, same hours but occasional overnights. I will also try new hours, a day shift. If it agrees with us, we will continue. If not, we will cut back. In either case, we would like to express our appreciation by giving you a raise. . . ." I paused.

No response came from Helga.

"We would appreciate . . . I would appreciate," I almost choked on these words; bile rose in my throat, but I continued, ". . . . if you would give us a hand for those occasional overnights. I will often be home . . . but your help . . . ."

She cut me off completely. "Do you want her at my house or here?" she asked.

So in theory, she was willing. "Whatever you prefer. I will not get in your way . . . I would love to spend time with Sara . . . An experienced woman, child care professional, would be a benefit even if I am home."

So I said it . . . Maybe she suspected . . . Who cared?

"Fine," she said. No more words were necessary. She rose and turned her back to me. She began the morning dishes. No money was discussed. We had always been generous.

Chapter 48

THAT WAS WHEN MRS. DENNY started breaking into my consciousness on a regular basis.

It was creepy. I got the promotion. My first day, I was nervous. After all, I could be social only to a point. I preferred to work alone.

As I stood in my new office, I heard her voice:

"God is your speedometer . . ."

The God thing didn't calm me down, but hearing her voice from the past did.

I sat down at my big desk. A pile of manuscripts were there with a note.

Assign these to your staff day or night.
You read only the ones your staff feels are worthy to pass on.
signed,
Eric Graham, Senior Editor and Chief

My desk faced the door. I could see everyone pass the glass partition in the hall.

I shifted my desk to the sidewall so I had more privacy. I buzzed my assistant Mrs. Percy.

She came in instantly. A gal after my own heart.

She was about sixty, fat, and competent with an annoying lisp.

"Please assign these manuscripts," I hesitated, as it was my first request.

Before I could say more, she was collecting them in her arms and leaving.

Now I had nothing to do.

I went through the files to see what already existed from my predecessor. That made me look busy when next she returned. "You have a meeting at noon. Lunch will be served with Mr. Graham." I rummaged through more files until noon.

When I arrived at noon, his office was packed with other staff members. Sandwiches were arranged on the side cabinet.

When we were all seated, he introduced me to the group.

I found this difficult. I didn't know what was expected of me. A speech?

Mrs. Denny's voice came clear in my head like a loudspeaker from the past, "Take joy in the ordinary . . . ."

This made me smile.

The group gave me a round of applause, then the boss was talking again.

My first day was factually easy but emotionally difficult. Thank goodness for Mrs. Denny.

THE NEXT FEW days were socially stressful but the work was about the same as nights. Maybe less because Mrs. Percy did almost everything. I was getting big bucks for doing less work.

I started getting up extra early. I'd feed Sara breakfast, cook up Helen's favorite: bacon, sausage and toast. Then I'd head out to the beach. The drive cleared my head. Most mornings I was there just as the sun came up.

I sat in the car or on a rock. I'd skim rocks across the water and feed the seagulls.

Sometimes, I'd throw a large piece of bread to one seagull. The others would chase him, grabbing it in midair.

As I sat there laughing at their foolishness, Mrs. Denny came again to me, her voice as clear as the day she stood next to me.

"Seeing the sun rise is like meeting God each morning."

As a boy, she had brought me to the beach to feed the seagulls. Somehow until that morning skimming rocks alone, I had forgotten.

I had slipped out early risking punishment and ignoring chores to meet her.

She put me on the handlebars of her bike and off we went. Looking back, I guess she was strong or I was scrawny.

The sun was coming up. We had sat in the sand long ago, the water lapping our toes, feeding seagulls and skimming rocks.

Chapter 49

HELEN FORGOT THAT AWFUL NIGHT in which I frightened her so. Thank God for His mercy in that regard.

Some weeks later I visited the doctor. Without details, I asked, "What does it mean when someone has wordless seizures, like flashbacks?"

"What behavior occurs?" she responded.

"Smelling smells, fists clenching, rapid eye movement, blacking out, that sort of thing . . .," I answered.

"Do they drink?" she asked.

"No, just occasionally," I added.

"Would this be someone you know?" she asked.

"No one in particular." I couldn't tell her.

"Oh." She was quiet for a long time, thinking. Then she answered, "I feel great sadness for such a person. They suffer wordlessly because of a trauma before they had language. Perhaps their minds shut down, but like a camera, the body and eyes made recordings. Even if they had language, the trauma entered at a non-verbal level." She was silent again.

I, too, was silent. I knew already what she said was so.

Hearing her gentle kindness filled me in a new way. Helen and I were both war veterans.

I looked into the doctor's eyes for the first time. I couldn't speak.

I fumbled for my money. My change fell. I descended to my knees to collect it.

She was wearing black lace-up shoes. My head hurt; something about them set my head spinning, or was it bending down?

She approached me.

The shoes were rising to kick me. I struck out, not seeing her.

Then she was stroking my head. I had fainted.

"The heat, my new job . . . ." I struggled for words.

She offered me some water and a tissue.

I regained my composure. "I have to go now," I said. I rushed out.

Chapter 50

THE FOLLOWING WEEK, HELEN STARTED teaching Sunday school at that lousy church where the pastor had upset me.

I decided it wasn't wise to go to the service anymore. But I did peek in on Helen's Sunday school class. She had fourth graders, twenty.

She was doing a lesson on Joseph and his coat of many colors. She had xeroxed line drawings that they were coloring.

One little girl was under the table and wouldn't came out. Since she was about nine years old, it seemed odd to me.

I got down on my knees to look at her under the table.

She started to cry, so I backed off.

Then I noticed her left ear was almost like a cauliflower ear. Reddened, swollen, the area behind it black and blue.

Could someone have hit her?

Or yanked on it?

It disturbed me.

Mercifully, Helen had completely forgotten that terrible night in which I went too far with her and Sara. I had a perverse audacity in being interested in this little girl when I had my own transgressions against humanity, right?

Nevertheless, I was curious. Maybe it pissed me off that this "holier-than-thou" congregation could have child abuse in its midst. Well, my dad went to church, right?

As we went to the diner afterwards, Sara was riding piggyback. We discussed Priscilla, the girl under the table.

"Oh, you're just reading too much into it," Helen said. "She could have banged into something . . . she may be shy, too. When you knelt down to her, a huge stranger, she just got frightened and cried, that's all."

What Helen said made sense, of course.

But similar to the judge, I smelled a rat. I had an instinct. Maybe it was because of my childhood, maybe because of my own proclivities.

Again, I became preoccupied. When I got home, I took some white fabric and cut a circle, glued it and stuffed it with cotton. I glued one piece of black yarn from Helen's crochet basket for hair; so it stood straight up from his head. I stiffened it with glue.

I took one of my old rugby shirts which was navy and red. I cut out a little shirt. Helen seamed up the sides and the head. She even sewed a white collar at the neck and put white hands on for me.

It was about eighteen inches in size. The head was six inches around. I made a "smiley" face, except I made a downward, slightly crooked frown, so he looked sad, not angry. With Helen's creativity, I had what I needed.

She was very curious about my intent. You know, I am handy with my hands, and I don't mean in my lovely games. I built the patio, the window molding, and many other things. As I mentioned, I had a plan.

Chapter 51

THE NEXT SUNDAY was Mother's Day. Helen and I never mentioned our own mothers. We did go for brunch. I got her a corsage or a little trinket and card. I picked up an ankle bracelet with tiny hearts. You could add more on the chain for each year or whatever. Since Helen had been a mother for four years, there were four tiny hearts, each stamped with a letter. Together, they spelled "SARA."

I also got a nice card, real schmoozy with satin ribbon.

I took her to brunch at this local greasy spoon that had a country western/folk singing group. We ordered pancakes drenched in blueberries and syrup.

But before lunch, I visited her Sunday school class with my puppet.

The little girl was under the table again. Helen's lesson was on Noah's Ark. The kids were coloring the animals to tape onto the large ark Helen had thumbtacked on the bulletin board.

Priscilla was in pigtails. Her dark hair was shiny. Two bows were yellow and checkered. Her dress was covered in applique daisies; around her waist was a yellow, checkered sash. She didn't look neglected, that was for sure. But you couldn't see inside.

I sat on the floor some distance from her.

Several kids came over in curiosity. I pretty much disrupted Helen's lesson. She got them back for singing "Old MacDonald Had a Farm." She called it "Old Man Noah Had an Ark."

I called my little puppet "Grouchy." I stuck him under the table with his hands covering his face.

I could see her ear was dry and peeling, but less swollen.

I had him with his face covered, then he slowly uncovered his face and tilted his head to look at her.

She smiled.

"Nobody loves me," Grouchy squeaked.

Her eyes opened wide, then she giggled."God loves you," she told him.

"No, God doesn't," he squeaked.

"Yes," she said, "Jesus loves you, even if no one else does," she whispered.

"Not me," Grouchy insisted. "'Cause I'm only two years old."

"I'm nine," she piped up.

"Jesus doesn't love me 'cause I'm funny looking," Grouchy explained.

"So am I," she responded, "But Jesus loves me, even if no one else does . . . ."

She was a beautiful child. So how had she come up with this?

"Who says," Grouchy asked.

"My mommy," she said. "She says I'm ugly and stupid, but I know God loves me . . . 'cause Helen said so."

Grouchy blew her a kiss. "Helen's right, and I think you're the prettiest, smartest girl I ever in my *whole* life met," Grouchy said.

The little girl smiled a sad smile and looked away.

"When I grow up, I'm going to marry you!" Grouchy squeaked.

"Really?" she asked.

"Yup," said Grouchy. "On account of the fact you're a secret princess."

This time she really beamed.

So like I said, we went for pancakes afterward. I gave Helen the ankle bracelet, the card, and the roses. It made me remember that day she picked them up at our diner in New York and pricked her little wing.

Mostly, I thought of little Priscilla. I knew I was right . . . .

Chapter 52

So I BEGAN "helping" Helen with her Sunday school class. We started planning the lesson together. Helen would get the Bible story and visual aids together. I came up with some story or humorous routine for Grouchy to do.

All I cared about was Priscilla. So I'd position myself on the floor next to her.

Pretty soon, she would come out from under, I hoped.

By the third week, her ear was almost healed, but there was a residual change in the lobe, which I doubted would go away. It stuck out slightly and was not shell-shaped anymore. It looked like a lump of clay somebody had tried to fashion into an ear.

She was a wounded vessel now, too. Just like my Helen, but more beautiful for the mark, which showed her survival of life's pain.

I'm not romanticizing her disfigurement, although it wasn't really that bad. I simply mean to me or any man who might see her in later life that she would hold an allure only the wounded can hold, just as bruises on Helen were attractive to me or her wing a treasure.

Similarly, her downcast eyes and uncertainty were marks. Her timidity said, "I have been cast aside. Am I worthy?"

To a man such as myself who could appreciate her, she would be a rare prize.

She would not cry out. She would willingly submit to be received fully as she was.

We were doing the Bible story, "The Pearl of Great Price." In it, a person finds a perfect pearl and casts aside all earthly treasures to obtain it alone.

It was perfect for Priscilla.

Helen got a little bag of pearls. She put each one in a tiny Plexiglas box and she placed a sticky back miniature bow on top.

Grouchy had an additional pearl for Priscilla, a secret.

I sat in my usual spot on the floor, but purposely a bit away.

I had Grouchy face Priscilla but speak more quietly than usual.

I cast my hook deep and I know how to wait.

When Helen had finished the story, a treasure hunt was announced.

"Each of you gets one prize," she said. "If you find a second prize, give it to someone still looking. Say, 'You are precious, you deserve a great prize.'"

So the hunt began.

Priscilla stayed under the table but inched close to me, her feet jutting out.

Grouchy pretended to look for his prize. I had "hidden" her prize conspicuously near me in a red shiny bag.

After searching for awhile, Grouchy and I sat down even further from Priscilla, still facing her.

"Did you find your treasure, Priscilla?" Grouchy asked. "It's there, Grouchy," she pointed near me.

"I don't see it," he answered.

She crawled out a little more. "There," she pointed again.

"Priscilla, is it on my head?" Grouchy squeaked.

Priscilla laughed. "No, silly." She crawled out more. "Right there!" she was fully out from the table now.

"Oh dear," said Grouchy, "nobody loves me, nobody wants to help me . . . ."

"I do, Grouchy," she grabbed the little bag. Then she hesitated to open it.

"May I sit with you?" Grouchy asked.

She nodded.

"Would you like to sit on my daddy's lap?" he asked.

She lifted her moist eyes almost pleadingly.

"May I?"

"Oh, sure you can," Grouchy said cheerfully.

Priscilla climbed right up on my lap.

Grouchy opened the bag for Priscilla. He took out the little treasure box. She gasped with delight.

"You are Precious Priscilla, you deserve a great prize," said Grouchy as he handed the little box to her.

She hugged his little puppet body to her.

"Oh Grouchy, I love you," she said.

"Oh Priscilla, I love you too," answered Grouchy.

"Will you marry me when I grow up?" he asked.

She nodded.

"You're my secret princess," Grouchy said.

When her mom and dad came, they yanked her out quickly by the elbow. They didn't even ask about the lesson or thank Helen.

WHEN I NEXT visited the doctor, I described Priscilla. "She will be some man's rare prize."

"Do you mean singled out for abuse or love?" the doctor asked.

I didn't understand her. "What? Love, of course."

"Well, would Priscilla or someone like Priscilla be more likely to accept pain and hurt as normal?"

"Well, I suppose." I hesitated.

"Might a potential abuser, a boyfriend or spouse, recognize what you did?" she asked.

I was dumbfounded. This had not occurred to me.

"You mean treasure her to hurt her?" I asked.

"Precisely." She was silent.

I pondered this a long time.

"What kind of person would deliberately seek or recognize this in her?" I was puzzled.

Her answer was slow and deliberate.

"Someone who had themselves been abused, I would say . . . ."

I saw lights dancing before my eyes, strobe lights flashing.

My temples throbbed. I struggled to maintain the moment. The moment passed.

I had forgotten the conversation. I stared blankly at the doctor.

"Priscilla?" she waited.

"She'll be fine," I said. I paid and left quickly.

Chapter 53

I STARTED WATCHING THE TEEN shelter, hoping to see the young fellow I dropped there.

I also called and left my beeper number so he could contact me. I reasoned he might remember me. Then again, he could come out schizophrenic and ready for a fix or drinking. I figured the beeper would require him to give a call-back number. I would be able to screen his situation.

I also started looking for him where I picked him up. Street people have patterns. They move in a two-mile radius usually. Even if he was rehabilitated, he might move in the same area. If his thing was prostitution or picking up men, he might continue even if he had a place to stay, even if he was detoxed.

Meanwhile, I continued to help Helen with her class. I was still drawn to Priscilla.

I was relieved when Priscilla's ear healed. I mentioned to Helen that I thought the church social worker should be told about it. Just in case.

Helen said she would call and mention it.

I'm a regular bleeding-heart liberal.

Sara was doing great in pre-kindergarten. She could count to twenty and say her ABC's. She was tracing her name and calendar numbers in school.

Helga actually stayed over only about once or twice a month. Helen's work schedule didn't much change in actual practice.

My work was easier than I expected, as Mrs. Percy was able to shield me from the necessary social aspects of my new job.

I decided to fix up the Manhattan apartment a little. I got a new bed and mattress. I repainted and added cheerful decor such as curtains, bedspreads, throw pillows, and a new recliner.

My whole episode with the judge had disquieted me.

I felt he had contaminated my space. This clean-up restoration helped. In fact, I even fumigated it.

Helen also did redecoration. Sara had outgrown the nursery. She now had a junior bed. The mobile we kept, because she still enjoyed it for her bedtime ritual. She added a chest of drawers. Sara now wore a larger size and had more changes of clothing, so Helen added hangers in the closet for her little dresses and shirts. Shelves and puzzle organizers, clear shoeboxes for blocks, tiny toys, a section for her library of picture books were also added. She even added an art area with an easel and plastic drop cloth, plus a rocking chair with a musical mechanism. All in all, it felt like we were entering a new phase together.

I put up a swing on the back for Sara. She would hold Puffy on her lap, singing him lullabies.

We were the picture of marital bliss.

Chapter 54

HELEN CALLED ME AT WORK to say there was a Church picnic on Sunday.

"Would you help with my class and bring Grouchy the puppet?"

"Sure." I was the milk of human kindness, don't you think?

Priscilla was there with her parents.

She was much different than I remembered her. With her parents she looked vacant, not there at all.

I approached her on the bus with Grouchy.

"Hi, Priscilla," Grouchy piped up.

She looked at him without recognition.

"Are you Priscilla?" he squeaked.

She shook her head. Her father laughed, but looked annoyed.

"She calls herself Leila now," he said.

"Really?" squeaked Grouchy.

"Yeah, she's more quiet since she decided she's Leila."

I doubted my little friend could be more withdrawn than I remembered her.

I went back to my seat furious, but I didn't know why.

Later at the picnic, Priscilla sat away from the group and her parents. She tossed pebbles into the little brook nearby. I approached her.

"Puddle jumpers . . .," Grouchy said.

Leila looked up past Grouchy, past me.

"The flat rocks help you cross without getting wet . . . They are puddle jumpers. Princess Priscilla can use them to get to the safe side," Grouchy said.

"She's gone," Priscilla answered, certain as can be.

As usual, my bait worked. My hook would sink deeper.

I waited. Grouchy covered his face and began to cry.

"Oh, my dearest, fairest Princess, my Priscilla. I miss her so very much," he sobbed.

In the purity of love, she opened her little arms to Grouchy. "Oh Grouchy, don't cry. I will take you to Priscilla . . ." she said.

Grouchy entered her arms, his face hidden in his tiny felt hands, still sobbing.

She held him tight to her heart. Then she started crying.

"I love you, Priscilla," Grouchy whispered.

"Oh Grouchy, I love you, too."

My little puppet and Priscilla quietly held each other.

"It's not safe here for you, Grouchy. Go," Priscilla warned. "If you stay here with me, they'll hurt you, too," she said.

"I have the magic of love," Grouchy answered.

"Oh, I need your magic, Grouchy. So bad," Priscilla said.

At that moment, her father started toward us.

"Leila, are you ready to go?" he asked sternly.

"May I cross the brook with Leila?" Grouchy asked.

"Her shoes will get wet," he answered.

Priscilla was dressed too formally for a picnic—patent leather shoes, a stiff transparent skirt of many layers, a yellow velvet top and satin sash. All were traps to prevent play.

"She can take her shoes off . . ., " Grouchy suggested.

"Are you challenging me?" her father asked me directly.

Priscilla changed before my eyes. Again, the vacant, far away look. Again the lack of recognition, then a radiant smile appeared. But Priscilla was gone.

"Leila wants Daddy to carry her back to sit with Mommy now," she announced.

I am a civilized man, but I am a man. In that moment I could have crushed his skull.

For Priscilla's sake, I played the game of civilization. For Helen, for Sara, I responded well.

"Grouchy will find you Princess, and Grouchy will protect you," my puppet answered.

Again, the grim-faced little girl returned. She blinked her eyes and nodded. Then she was gone.

I returned to Helen. My temples throbbed. I could feel the heat in my face. My fists pulsated. My heart beat loudly. I was wild with killer lust.

Helen's eyes opened wide in horror to see me. She slipped her one hand over my fist and her little wing into my other. I could not unclench them. Sara was dangling her feet in the water with another child.

She kissed my eyes. They flew open because to close them was to go backward in time. Yet to open them was to murder. Only blood could satisfy.

It was then Helen began to cry and buried her head in my chest.

For the moment, her pain obliterated Priscilla's and my own.

Chapter 55

THAT NIGHT I AGAIN SUFFERED kidney pain. I soaked in a hot tub and sipped hot tea. Helen awoke and massaged my lower back. Even the painkillers didn't help. Helen took my temperature. It was 104 degrees. I shuddered; chills coursed through my legs.

Helen called Helga. She was there by the time we were dressed.

I couldn't tie my shoes. The pain blocked my ability to think straight. Helen even helped me with my underwear. She drove to the medical center.

I was hooked to an intravenous drip of painkillers and antibiotics for six hours.

I "tripped" psychotically, rolling in and out of dreams and hallucinations. The nurse wore a hideous clown mask, then melted away. Helen said I pushed her to the floor. The doctor came to give me an injection and I saw a butcher knife in its place.

Helen said they had to tie me down. They called it toxic uremia from the backed-up urine.

I know the infection was Priscilla's father.

I was discharged after six hours. The next few hours at home I rested. Helen disrobed me.

During the night, a scarecrow oozing pus and blood carried me off. I felt crows pecking at my eyes and my genitals.

I grew bigger and bigger until I held the world in my fist. I crushed it with my hands; blood trickled through my fingers.

At last I could have peace in the dream. All was dead, even me. I awoke to find my legs and arms bound to the bed.

During the night I had some kind of breakdown. Helen had become frightened, I guess.

When I awoke, my rage returned. How dare she do this to me?

Sweetly, I called out to her.

"Helen, my angel, my love, won't you come here?"

No answer.

I bellowed at the top of my lungs.

"Bitch! Lousy, deceitful bitch, untie me!" No answer came.

Then I came to my senses. I moved my head over to my wrist and undid the knot with my teeth.

I was free.

A note on the refrigerator said,

Be right back, Helen

How was I supposed to read this if I was bound to the bed upstairs? Did she expect me to release myself?

Or was that too only the imagination of my diseased kidney?

When Helen returned with Sara, she was cheerful, almost lighthearted. Not to say she wasn't concerned about my kidney, but she made no reference to my need to be tied to the bed.

So I asked her.

"Why did you tie me to the bed during the night?"

Her face flushed bright red, then drained of all color.

"But how could I restrain you? You're so big . . . and here you are free . . . ." She seemed genuinely flustered.

I decided it was my delirium from the toxins and ghosts. But despite her reassurances, I was inexplicably restless and enraged.

I knew it wasn't Helen. God knows she was my only peace on earth.

Sara's birthday was the next day.

Helen had gone out to get party favors and ingredients for a chocolate cake. She happily busied herself in the kitchen, letting Sara assist her. Sara could break the eggs into a bowl, add oil, and best of all, use the electric mixer.

She giggled with delight to see it mix everything together.

Then they scooped it into heart shaped pans. Sara's dress and Helen's were of the same fabric. Helen had made them and several others for the summer.

Sara was a miniature Helen; her little throat, embellished with a replacement cross I had given her, was almost translucent. She had star shaped gold stud earrings. Her hair was pulled back into a high ponytail with a bright pink ribbon that matched with the tiny rose print on her dress. Helen, too, had pulled her hair back in a ponytail. Her neck was adorned with a gold locket I had given her after the cruise. Inside I had put our pictures.

"I'll give Sara her bath," I announced.

I grabbed her and set her on my shoulders. I ran up the stairs two at a time. I held her supple thighs to balance her.

Her dark eyes and lashes were bright with excitement.

She could undress herself, of course. She would be five the next day. Her shoes were slip-on sneakers with Minnie Mouse on each toe.

She scrambled out of her clothes as I drew a bubble bath for her. She had an assortment of rubber animals for the tub and could busy herself for up to an hour playing and chattering to them.

I was in my robe still. I sat on the edge and I dangled my feet into the tub.

I made a game of tickling her with my toes. I scrubbed her back, skimming her backside a little. Then I suggested we wash her hair.

She closed her eyes and stood up so I could lather and rinse her. The spray nozzle I had added to the tub allowed me to quickly rinse her hair. As the suds slipped down her delicate body, I could see the pleasure she could give me already.

I squirted the water between her legs to rinse her, and then sensing the danger zone I had entered, left her to play by herself.

Helen was just frosting the cake when I returned. I lifted the remaining frosting from the bowl with my fingers. She too began to scoop out chocolate frosting. I suddenly remembered that fateful day I had escaped the basement and reentered our family unit. How I had drugged them both flashed before me and how Sara had thrown chocolate pudding at me, somehow introducing humor into the difficult moment.

Helen's lips were smeared with chocolate. Even a little rested on her shoulder somehow.

I licked her mouth and shoulder and opened my robe. I guided her out to the swing.

"But Sara," she protested.

"She takes forever," I reassured her.

I lay her down on the swing, placing a pillow beneath her head. On impulse I put one under her bottom. Then I fastened the scarves around her four limbs.

Again she protested, "But Sara."

"I'll put her to bed."

I went upstairs. Sara still played.

"Bed time, my sweetheart."

"I want Mommy," she said.

"She'll be right up. She sent you some chocolate frosting." I gave her a little cup and spoon with a dollop of the sweet frosting. I had mixed her Benadryl into it. She brushed her teeth. I read her a silly story called "Hop on Pop" by Dr. Seuss. She was groggy when we finished. I took her into bed. As I left her room, I felt a demon take hold of me. I retraced my steps and lifted her blanket, then I raised her nightdress. A little peek wouldn't harm her, I reasoned. She didn't wake up. I touched her delicately, just barely sliding my fingers through her legs.

She groaned. I quickly covered her again. I turned on her carousel night-light and closed her door.

Helen was still submissively waiting for me. Well, what choice did she have? My problem was I hadn't sedated her. Nevertheless, she trustingly waited. I went into the kitchen and got the remaining frosting. I made a game of licking a little and feeding her some, until her dose was finished. Then I stroked her head, her shoulders and arms. I slipped down her dress straps. Her scar was barely visible now. Her milky breasts spilled out of her pink lace bra.

Her underwear matched. It was easy to just slide it to the side and tenderly continue to stroke her. When I reached her feet, she was asleep.

I knew I held a demon at bay. Upstairs with Sara, I had felt its presence.

I knew too well the rage I was capable of. The vividness of the dreams while at the hospital, the looming face of my father and Priscilla mixed with my lingering question. Could Helen have actually tied me to my own bed? It was ludicrous, of course, but my rage wasn't rational.

I untied her and carried her to the basement. Tonight I didn't care if she resisted. I would just sedate her more. I laid her on the examination table. I slipped another Valium under her tongue and waited. I fondled her and gently kissed her.

I stripped off my robe and lifted my weights. As usual, the sight of my own body excited me.

Then I returned to Helen. I raised her skirt and slipped off her panties. I put her tiny feet into the metal stirrups and slid her down to the edge of the table. No resistance this time. Enough sedation, I supposed.

I placed my lamp near and focused on her delicate parts and began to open her, to inspect her, to study her, to study what was rightfully mine.

Her eyes flew open. Her head raised. She looked right at me. Her pupils were dilated. Then she collapsed back.

I nearly fainted. Now I was really pissed off. But something deeply humbling caused me to remove her from the table and take her upstairs to our bed.

I tilted her over several pillows, my rage taking over. I believe I entered her in more than one way. When I was finished, a peace settled over me.

Hell, I could examine her anywhere, couldn't I?

I trained the table lamp toward her. I was ashamed and pleased with my work. She oozed my fluids mixed with blood. My dear sweet Helen had calmed me again. And perhaps, who knows; others, at least for that night, had been spared.

Chapter 56

A FEW DAYS LATER, I RETURNED to work. You know, the sameness of routine brought me back some equilibrium. I was following a constant water-drinking routine. All I did was edit, drink water, and piss.

I developed an eccentricity around this time.

I visited my senior editor and asked the ridiculous.

"Sir, I wonder if you would allow me to bring my cat into work? He is very good and he reduces my stress . . . ." I felt foolish.

"No problem. You produce, you get what you want. I bring my dog in sometimes. Just run it by our mutual boss . . . Mrs. Percy." He winked.

So I began driving into work with "Kitty Business." No one knew except my senior editor and Mrs. Percy.

She thought it was "simply charming."

It calmed my nerves and brought a domestic aura into my work place.

My kidneys were being monitored weekly. I had a urine tester at home. I was to test the acidity and dilution.

I called Bellevue the week I got back to work. "John Doe," my little friend, had been held. I spoke to the social worker. She gave me the usual line about confidentiality. I asked if she could try to get him into the upstate facility run by the monks. She said she was working on a residential treatment facility for Runaways in Poughkeepsie, New York. I got the phone number of the pay phone on the unit and called him. He was using the name "Bill Smith," still, I think.

"Yeah, who's this?" he screamed into the phone.

"A concerned friend," I said.

"I don't got no friends, mister, just tricks," he answered. "What's your angle? I'm trying to get myself together. Ain't a guy allowed any peace, even in the hospital?" he pleaded.

He was right. I had used him just like any trick.

"I'm glad you're taking care of yourself. Since you're doing that, I'll leave you alone . . ." I lingered on the phone.

"Mister, you the one who brought me to the hospital?" he asked.

I hesitated.

"They said I could have died. I had alcohol and Valium mixed with my other medicines . . . So thanks." Now he hesitated.

I had almost killed my little friend. The Valiums, after all, had been my doing. He didn't know that. He also didn't know I had relieved myself and fondled him before rescuing him.

Anyway, I finally said, "I'll send money, no strings attached, care of your social worker. If you get straight . . . ."

No answer came.

Finally, he spoke.

"So I'm alert when you play your little games?" he rasped in a sob.

Then he hung up.

I'M A REASONABLE GUY MOST of the time. I think you would agree. Yet, I do believe my entire kidney episode was precipitated by stress.

Priscilla's father visited my thoughts at night and occasionally at work. The cat helped. Just stroking him as I read my manuscripts was soothing.

Priscilla's father's hateful, disturbing presence was an underpinning to everything I did. It was as if there was only room enough in my weary psyche for so many ghosts.

My adaptive energy was running out. The spooks were winning. If it wasn't my father it was Priscilla's father.

I needed to perform an exorcism. I needed to rid myself at least of Priscilla's father.

It wasn't altruism for Priscilla's plight. My sanity depended on knowing one less goon was out there. I was spending too much emotional energy managing my rage and suppressing my flashbacks.

I drove to Priscilla's house early one morning and watched her father leave at five in the morning. I followed

Chapter 57

I MADE AN APPOINTMENT TO see my therapist.

"I just wondered," I asked, "if a child is mistreated by her father, does it have to be physical to have him removed from the home?"

"Can you be more specific?" she asked.

I outlined Priscilla's behavior of withdrawing under the table. I described her swollen ear. I described her peculiar behavior on the picnic.

"She definitely seems stressed, but you may be reading too much into it." She waited for me to react.

"Well, he seems to be upsetting her badly," I said.

"Well yes, but you may also be seeing yourself in Priscilla's situation." She paused.

"How could I get a social worker involved in the case?" I asked.

"You don't have any specifics, but you could call in an anonymous complaint with the Bureau of Child Welfare and they would open a file. If just your complaint comes in, it would be closed again." She waited.

My idea was now taking on a better form. By the time I left the doctor's office, I had a plan.

I ALREADY KNEW where Priscilla's father worked. On an impulse, I decided to try my luck at implementing my plan.

I pretended to bump into him outside his building after work. I apologized for my "behavior" at the picnic. I blamed the use of the puppet. He grumbled but accepted it. I offered to get him a drink.

"There's a bar that offers free appetizers," I suggested. They offered "pigs in a blanket." They were miniature franks with doughy crusts. I had several with me that I had already put sedatives into.

When he went to the bathroom, I asked for more at our table and put mine among them. As he sat down, he ate the drugged hot dogs.

Then I looked at my watch. "Oh my goodness," I said, "Look at the time." He picked up on the cue. I paid the check. I had parked my car near his in the parking lot. When he got there I tried to start my car. Of course, it didn't start. I honked my horn.

"Gee, I hate to impose but, well, I think my car is dead. Could you give me a lift? I'm going to a business appointment at the Washington Hotel."

He didn't look pleased, but he grudgingly gave me a ride.

I had already gotten two rooms. One was Room 28; the other was Room 30. At my request, he came up for a moment.

"I need to be certain I can get a car service home later," I explained. I busied myself on the phone calling various car services. After about fifteen minutes, he slumped in the armchair.

I left him quickly and drove his car to Twenty-third Street and Ninth Avenue. I picked up a girl of about fifteen who was wearing a black garter belt and mesh stockings, but no skirt. She had her red coat opened. She jumped into my car. I gave her fifty dollars. She started to unzip my pants but that wasn't my game.

We drove to the hotel. I took her upstairs to Room 28.

I explained this was an old high school buddy. "He's beat from the plane ride. But you would be a welcome wake-up call," I said. She seemed pleased with this. I ordered up champagne and brought out brownies for us to munch with it.

She downed most of the champagne and brownies. When she had ingested enough of my special brownies, she too passed out. I removed her clothing and his, then positioned them in the bed. I put his hands up her vagina and his head on her breasts.

Then I left. Then I washed up in Room 30. Finally, I left the hotel and called the police from a pay phone.

"My daughter is only fifteen," I quivered into the phone. She went to meet her teacher . . .Yes, her high school teacher. I couldn't stop her . . . They're at the Hotel Washington. Please help me." I gave a fictitious address and name, but correctly identified "her teacher."

"I heard her say Room 28 I think . . . ." Then I hung up the phone. I took a bus back to my car and drove home.

I was again a happy man.

The local papers carried the story.

"Local businessman using drugs lures teenage girl."

I figured this, with my previous phone call to the Bureau of Child Welfare, would nix his little attitude with Priscilla.

Chapter 58

PRISCILLA'S DAD DIDN'T RETURN TO the church, but her mother and she did. Helen and I continued to plan the lessons. I was peripheral to the content, most times. Grouchy and I were comic relief.

Priscilla was absent for three weeks when the case made the papers. I guess her mom was embarrassed. Surprisingly, the fourth week, they did come back.

For the first time since I had met Priscilla some eight months before, she sat on a chair, of course, next to Grouchy.

Grouchy spoke first.

"Hi Leila," he said.

"Leila's gone away," Priscilla answered.

"Oh, she's gone?" repeated Grouchy.

"I'm back, Grouchy," Priscilla announced.

"I love you, Priscilla," Grouchy immediately answered.

"I love you, Grouchy." Priscilla hugged Grouchy.

"Do you love Leila?" she asked cautiously.

"I love all of you—Priscilla, Leila too," Grouchy answered without hesitation.

"All of me?" she said, savoring this idea.

"Leila's part of me, right?" she asked.

"Isn't she Priscilla?" Grouchy squeaked.

"She likes to help," Priscilla answered matter-of-factly.

Grouchy nodded. "That's why I love her too. She's your helper and I love you." Grouchy stroked her cheek with his little felt hand.

"Oh Grouchy," Priscilla hugged Grouchy's hand.

Well, I admit my psychological intervention with her father was a little unconventional. But hell, it worked.

WHEN PRISCILLA'S MOM picked her up, she was really tense. She just yanked her out.

Helen and I doing a Sunday school class was pretty funny, right? I figured if there was a damn God, God was in Priscilla's smile or in my Helen.

God was never in my dad or mom. But maybe in my beautiful Helen or my dog Lucky.

There was a purity to the animals, wasn't there? I mean, did they show hidden agendas or ever betray me?

Okay, the whole Fluffy thing was disastrous. Who was that guy who killed Fluffy anyway? Had I sent him away for good when I stopped drinking?

No matter how I looked at it, I still didn't like Fluffy, not even in memory. So I guess I was still confused. But Priscilla, Helen, they didn't confuse me. They were pure in my mind, and if there was anything to this crap Helen was teaching, it lay somewhere in their eyes.

Chapter 59

I PASSED MY LITTLE RENEGADE waif, the boy I had taken to Bellevue again about a month later. He was diseased again. His face was erupting in muscle spasms and spittle. He was screaming profanities while sipping his beer on a stoop. Another homeless guy was screaming at him.

My little friend had stumbled out of a candy store without paying for his roll.

"You'll be punished. You can't just do things like that. It's wrong. It's blasphemy," the old blonde man screamed.

"Stick it where the squirrel puts its nuts," my little friend screamed, unperturbed. He stood and grabbed his crotch and shook it at the old man.

The old man waved his hand in frustration through the air and went on his way. So my crazy friend was back to square one again. I studied him through the window of a parked van across the street.

It was interesting how he was always in this same two-block radius. Maybe he had a history in this neighborhood. Maybe there was a shelter. I watched him for a while but he had a hyper-vigilance about him despite how gone he appeared. He actually started looking in the general direction of the van as if he felt himself being watched. So I left.

Could you force someone to be well? Was I similarly diseased, but in a cleaner wrapper?

I dropped into a lunchtime A.A. meeting. The old man I had met before was there. I approached him before the meeting started.

I didn't go through social preliminaries. I didn't know how. I got right to it.

"Mister," I asked, "I know a kid, a teenager. He drinks, does drugs, and is deluded. What can I do?"

"Let go, let God, son," he said. "Give it over to your Higher Power. Know the things you can change and the things you can't." He pulled the Serenity Prayer out of his pocket and gave it to me. He picked his tooth with his pinky and spat something out to his side.

"Just like that," he said. "Get rid of it. You got no business micro-managing all of God's fucking creation."

I sat down as if he had punched me in the chest. He had taken the wind out of me.

"Let go, let God," he repeated. "Work your program." He meant the twelve steps of A.A.

The meeting started. I left. I had gotten what I needed.

I LOOKED AT MYSELF IN the mirror at work. I looked at my dimples and the real white hair. I had left it in with the fake blonde tint. I looked at myself through my fake blue eyes.

I had always used false costumes and disguises, since I had left the farm. My foster parents knew me by an alias. I now used their name as an alias. I had covered my tracks as a habit most of my adult life. "Let go; let God" needed some translation or transposition.

Let go; let roots show in my hair? Let go; reveal eye color? Let go; uncover my dirty little tracks, my many deceits?

That was carrying the A.A. thing a bit too far, don't you think?

I'm a reasonable man. I like choices, plenty of choices.

If I needed to bail out of my marriage, just pop out my lenses. If I did something a little adventuresome, did I really want it out there for the general public to know? Did I want to be arrested?

Hell, no.

And I wasn't ready to give up my games. I would just go "one day at a time" as they said, even with their damn program.

I wasn't finished with the waif boy exactly, but for now, I could see it was not as appealing as I had thought.

Chapter 60

A FEW NIGHTS LATER I was at home working on the computer. For a few minutes I went into the chat room. Someone said press "911" on my keyboard for extra fun, so I did. I'm not usually so open, but I figured what the hell, since we were in cyberspace. Next thing I knew the doorbell rings and the police are there.

The precinct emergency screen and all car computers for this vicinity were flashing our address and an emergency signal. Just what I needed, right?

We reassured them but they still wanted to look around. After they left, one half hour later, it happened again. The doorbell rang. They said they had been called once more.

This continued to occur six times up until midnight. Now what I really didn't need was the police investigating me. I really didn't need them looking around the root cellar and into my past, right? I was shaken up pretty badly. Frankly, so was Helen.

The first time a guy came to the door who was the size of a little kid in a police uniform. I nearly cracked up laughing. But of course, I didn't dare. This was real and could ruin everything for me. The second time four cops came. The spokesman for the group was tall as me, fat and arrogant. It took all my patience to remain charming, concerned, and quizzical.

They looked at the computer and suggested I shut it down and not use it for a few days. Hell, I'm canceling my subscription to the chat rooms. They didn't have to warn me about the risks or imminent threat implied in this cute little cyberspace joke. Some idiot was able to hack into the police emergency computer and find my address through the phone lines. Then they sent a distress call to distress me. Now I understood. It could be a kid in Wyoming or China. Cyberspace or chat rooms were international phone lines. But I felt personally threatened.

Suppose they got a warrant to search our place? Suppose they began surveillance of our house? Also, who was the wise guy who picked me?

Helen was very shaken by the whole thing. Puffy was barking the whole time and wouldn't shut up, even when they left. Sara woke up and couldn't fall back to sleep until past two in the morning. The doorbell and the dog barking woke her.

In a way it helped the situation that I was holding Sara in my arms when they came the second time. She was crying. I guess she remembered in some vague way the night of the fire.

We looked like the picture of domestic bliss—Sara in my arms, Puffy barking and Helen by my side.

The sixth time it happened, they came with three squad cars. I didn't think this small town even owned three police cars. A pimple-faced volunteer in a police uniform recognized Helen from church.

"Don't you teach Sunday School over at First Church?" she asked.

"Yes, I do," Helen answered.

This helped get them off our back, too. I decided to lay low for a while. Real low.

Chapter 61

I CONTINUED TO TRAVEL TO and from work with Kitty Business. He would sit on my lap the whole drive there. It was very soothing. I had sabotaged myself at work in a way. I was too good at my job and my boss called me into his office a few months after my promotion.

"I want to make you the area director," he announced.

"What does that entail?" I asked.

"Well, for one thing, negotiating contracts for books, printing costs, setting up book signings." His voice trailed off.

My heart was racing. This kind of high profile job would kill me. I might be recognized. It was social on a regular basis. I tried to regroup. My chest was tight.

"I'm actually a real family man. I'm concerned about the impact on my marriage that such a job might bring," I responded tentatively.

"Oh, you'd be called out of town infrequently. You could travel with your wife if necessary. Ms. Percy would continue with you and travel if you requested her," he volunteered.

"But wouldn't there be more social and time demands?" I asked.

"Just a shift. You could be as public or private as you liked," he said.

"But I like the hands-on of editing, you know, reading the raw manuscripts," I said. I think I was almost pleading.

"Oh, sure you do," he urged. "But you'll still do that. You'll read them for final decisions, based on your support team's recommendations. You'll decide on the commercial value of a book in negotiating a price," he continued.

"But I've never done that," I responded.

"I'll give you one month of transition time and work with you. Then I'll cut you loose. You'll find your way just like I did," he chuckled.

I was scared out of my mind. "What if I say no?" I asked.

"Then I axe you," he answered. "I'm reorganizing the company," he smiled magnanimously. "You'll be fine," he finally said.

WHAT I WAS really worried about was my stress level. If it got high enough, my rage surfaced. Then kaput, a wild card was almost always my next step. I could barely handle my stress as it was. With the police episode I needed to really lay low. Let's face it, I didn't need the money. My job was a lifestyle choice. I had an excuse for coming and going. If I used my parents or foster parents' income in any visible way, I would have to explain my past to Helen and my previous identities.

I knew if I was fired, I could regroup. So I decided to give the new job a try. It would be an inconvenience, maybe even dangerous given my nature. But life had dealt me tougher blows.

THE TRANSITION MONTH was strange. My boss gave me ideas and pumped me for ideas. We spent too much time together. At one point it was laughable. He brought in his golden retriever. I had my cat. It could have been our living room, we were so comfy and "down home." The first time he walked into my office with his dog and saw my cat he froze. His dog padded up to Kitty and sniffed him, then collapsed clumsily on the floor. He ordered in pizza for us. We worked through lunch. The dog stole my slice off the plate. The cat stole his anchovies.

Well, I figured, maybe this wouldn't be so bad after all.

Chapter 62

I WAS NOT PREPARED FOR what happened that next weekend. As I have said, I never meant to hurt Helen and certainly not Sara. Like the man said, it's not all under my control.

Helen had stayed at church to meet with some other teachers at the Sunday School. Sara rode home with me. Puffy had vomited up on the kitchen floor, those hair ball things. I guess the heat was hitting him, too.

I peeled off everything but my underwear. I stripped Sara to hers, her face was too flushed. We sat to drink lemonade freezes from the blender. Watching her run back and forth across the kitchen floor with Puffy chasing her was fun. I had been reviewing her videos from infancy and was intrigued by all of her changes. From the behind her bottom now arched back like Helen's. Her shoulders formed an inverted triangle to her narrow waist and hips. She was wearing those little ruffled panties only girls can wear in our culture. Helen got them to match with her dresses and socks. Even her socks had lace trim. Looking back, I wonder, should I have undressed her as I did?

I see it all in my mind's eye in slow motion. Sara on tiptoes, tilted into the kitchen counter, pivoted as a ballerina doll on one toe, then moving after Puffy, her glass in her tiny hand. It was slow motion. I was frozen in place, unable to move. Was it fascination or the rapidity with which it all happened that rendered me a viewer in a tragedy?

As she turned, the glass fell. She slipped backward, simultaneously crashing onto the already broken glass.

Screams came and blood from her behind and front. I stood riveted in place, not realizing I was an actor in this drama. Then her screams broke through.

I was lifting her, seeing shards of glass glistening on her inner thighs, feeling them on her buttocks even as I lifted her. And Sara wriggling, writhing, shrieking, "Daddy, oh Daddy, help me!"

I carried her over to the first aide box in the pantry closet, yanked peroxide and cotton, all in a dream. Her eyes were wild with pain. Even as I lifted her, I shoved the shards further into her genitals and buttocks and my own hands. Too late to change strategies; I flipped her to hold her waist and brought her to the porch, the sunlight and the bonds. She was thrashing in a tantrum of terror. No reasoning was left in her or me. My knees were jello with trembling; my heart raced, dots appeared before my eyes and I struggled not to pass out.

I talked her through my strategy, but she suddenly went limp in my arms. Was an artery severed? Had her mind collapsed to protect her from the pain and terror? I lay her limp on the porch swing. I tied the bonds, her legs splayed, her face down. My hands were shaking as I ran back to get scissors from the kitchen drawer. Then I cut her underwear off, delicately pulling vertically in the hopes of dislodging the shards of glass.

Her bottom free, I doused peroxide over her, avoiding her genitals. I poured water over her inner parts to clear a visual area. Had I not done so many experiments in my childhood, perhaps I would have lost all presence of mind. I gently glided the wet cotton over her genitals. To my horror, the cotton caught on the jagged edges of pieces too horribly intimate with her small anatomy. Perspiration ran across my brow into my eyes and momentarily blinded me. When I regained my focus, I heard a gasp. Again, in slow motion, I turned. Helen stood at the porch door, her mouth open, her hand flying to cover a scream.

A backwards still-frame action flicked in my head. Helen moved backward into the kitchen. Glue in my veins, I followed, unable to articulate the situation.

"It's not what you think, Helen," I pleaded. I believe I was crying. She certainly was, even as she backed away from me. She stiffened, moving suddenly in fast frame, like a sped-up cartoon. Then she had the rifle in her good arm with the trigger held, her tiny wing supporting its weight.

It was over instantly. I crumbled to the floor, still pleading for mercy and her love.

She pulled me to the hated cellar door and tipped me with her foot over the edge. "Mommy knows what to do . . . Mommy knows what to do," was all she kept repeating. She wasn't seeing me at all anymore.

Then a crash, my bones crunching under me and blackness.

My heart was broken, is broken, as I write. How long can I go on in this way, again a prisoner? Again trapped in the prison of my childhood? My heart aches more than my ribs or ruined legs. Am I mortally wounded? Will the police finally come to take me away, to lock me in the dungeon of my past? Will the gloved wonder still be waiting in some corner of reality or my consciousness?

My only loves are ripped from me. I am horrid. No more a man but a monster to be flushed away, so all trace of union is gone.

If there is a God, I pray to you now: "Give me back my Helen. Give me back my dream. I am penitent. I am a convert. Because light is preferable to darkness, love preferable to horror. If this is how it finally ends, oh God, if you are a God, grant me love again."

DON'T MISS THIS BOOK . . .

Family Secrets

Meet the Grandees, the one family that epitomizes America's dark underside of violence, bigotry, adultery, alcoholism and poverty. They have all but lost their spirit and are in danger of losing their souls.

Caught between the onslaught of the Great Depression and an impending World War, the Grandees, like the extraordinary nation they live in, will either gather themselves together to triumph or succumb to the most sinister forces of human nature.

"THE BEST HISTORICAL NOVEL I'VE READ IN YEARS. Carefully researched and beautifully written, Father, Dear Father marks the beginning of a promising literary career for Mr. Reinherz. With an unerring feel for the period, and a cast of vividly drawn characters, this remarkable author has created a plot that astounds and delights by turn. One can only hope for a sequel."

– John Pellicano, author of *Conquer or Die*

"Reinherz has crafted an intriguing story of one man's sins and survival; reminding us that life's darkest torments are surmountable and life's triumphs all the richer when shouldered as a family. shared with true friends and supported in a spiritual community."

– Rebekah F. Witter, award-winning author of
Living with HorsePower!;
Rugged Lark, America's Super Horse;
and Riata Ranch Cowboy Girls

"ABSOLUTELY GORGEOUS! The writing is deft, the plot is electric, and I swear I felt CATAPULTED BACK IN TIME!"

– Betsy Hallet-Holden, author of *Nantucket's Night Magic*

AND COMING SOON . . .

A FAMILY AFFAIR

by Arthur Reinherz

"A tough, mature, brilliantly paced novel of scintillating characters and cinematic plot."

— Walter E. Williams, author, *Love Without Limit*

This is the extraordinary saga of a Jewish family in New England during the first half of the twentieth century. A compelling tale depicted through parallel love affairs, told against the backdrop of America—and a world—in bloody turmoil.

Albert Diamond, a house-to-house peddler makes the mistake of falling passionately in love with a Catholic girl, Joyce Neely whose father is just as adamant as the Diamonds to destroy the relationship—even if it means violence or murder.

Adam Diamond is drawn into a relationship with Beth, the beautiful, captivating daughter of an English Lord and eventually finds himself thrust into the front-lines of the Second World War.

From the Depression-era streets of Boston to the war-torn villages of Burma, A FAMILY AFFAIR follows the members of the indefatigable Diamond family from the late twenties through the end of World War II and its aftermath. It is a book that will stay with you forever.

"*A Family Affair* is that rare find: literary soap opera and period fiction at it's very best. Evocative, detailed, lovingly rendered with plenty of action, exotic locales and fascinating characters. Move over Sheldon, Uris, Steele, and Shaw. There's a new guy on the block and his name is Reinherz."

— Rev. Billie Marie Zal, author, *The Fabric of our Lives*

"A compelling portrait of Americans through poverty, war, and their eventual triumphs. *A Family Affair* is a masterpiece."

— W. Schoollkopf, author, *New York Measure*

About the Author

Remington Rose is an ordained minister and therapist and who has served in churches and worked in psychiatric and clinical settings for over 20 years in the Greater New York area.